Victor J. Daley

At Dawn and Dusk

Victor J. Daley

At Dawn and Dusk

ISBN/EAN: 9783337377748

Printed in Europe, USA, Canada, Australia, Japan

Cover: Foto ©Andreas Hilbeck / pixelio.de

More available books at **www.hansebooks.com**

AT DAWN AND DUSK

BY

VICTOR J. DALEY

SYDNEY
ANGUS AND ROBERTSON
PUBLISHERS TO THE UNIVERSITY
1898

Sydney: Websdale, Shoosmith and Co., Printers

TO MY SISTER

In memory of our young days ashine
  With dreams, when life was yet an opening rose,
Take, Alice dear, this little book of mine,
  All made of dreams and dying sunset-glows,
A lonely bird that singeth far apart—
Yet shall sing sweeter in its home, thy heart.

.

Almost all the verses contained in this volume were first published in the Sydney *Bulletin :* others appeared in the Sydney *Mail,* Sydney *Freeman's Journal,* Melbourne *Table Talk,* and *Melbourne Punch.* I wish to thank the editors and proprietors of these journals for their kindness in allowing me to reprint them.

V. J. D.

CONTENTS

x.   CONTENTS

CONTENTS

DREAMS

I HAVE been dreaming all a summer day
Of rare and dainty poems I would write;
Love-lyrics delicate as lilac-scent,
Soft idylls woven of wind, and flower, and stream,
And songs and sonnets carven in fine gold.

The day is fading and the dusk is cold;
Out of the skies has gone the opal gleam,
Out of my heart has passed the high intent
Into the shadow of the falling night—
Must all my dreams in darkness pass away?

I have been dreaming all a summer day:
Shall I go dreaming so until Life's light
Fades in Death's dusk, and all my days are spent?
Ah, what am I the dreamer but a dream!
The day is fading and the dusk is cold.

A   ı

DREAMS

My songs and sonnets carven in fine gold
Have faded from me with the last day-beam
That purple lustre to the sea-line lent,
And flushed the clouds with rose and chrysolite;
So days and dreams in darkness pass away.

I have been dreaming all a summer day
Of songs and sonnets carven in fine gold;
But all my dreams in darkness pass away;
The day is fading, and the dusk is cold.

LETHE

THROUGH the noiseless doors of Death
Three passed out, as with one breath.

Two had faces stern as Fate,
Stamped with unrelenting hate.

One upon her lips of guile
Wore a cold, mysterious smile.

Each of each unseen, the pale
Shades went down the hollow vale

Till they came unto the deep
River of Eternal Sleep.

Breath of wind, or wing of bird,
Never that dark stream hath stirred;

3

Still it seems as is the shore,
But it flows for evermore

Softly, through the meadows wan
To the Sea Oblivion.

In the dusk, like drops of blood,
Poppies hang above the flood;

On its surface lies a thin,
Ghostly web of mist, wherein

All things vague and changing seem
As the faces in a dream.

Two knelt down upon the bank
And of that dark water drank.

But the Third stood by the while,
Smiling her mysterious smile.

Rising up, those shades of men
Gazed upon each other, then

Side by side, upon the bank,
In a bed of poppies sank.

" What," one to the other saith,
" Sent *thee* through the doors of death ?"—

" While life throbbed in every vein,
  For a woman I was slain.

" Love is but a fleeting spell,
  Hate alone remembers well.

" For my slayer I shall wait,
  And though he at Heaven's gate

" Stand, and wear an angel's crown,
  I shall seize and drag him down ! "

So the stern shade made reply.
Then the first that spake said : " I

" For a woman's sake, also,
  Slew myself—and slew my foe.

" Slew myself, that in no shape
  He my vengeance should escape,

" Till Oblivion swallow both :
  And I swore a solemn oath

5

"I would—hate remembers well—
Hunt his spotted soul to hell.

"But I left, ere leave-taking,
Round her throat a dark red ring.

"I shall know her—you shall note—
By that red ring round her throat.

"Well I loved my fair, false wife,
And perchance in this new life

"She may love me—we shall see—
She shall choose 'twixt him and me."

Softly did the other sigh :
"My love's love will never die.

"Love is *not* a fleeting spell—
Love, like hate, remembers well.

"Soon—mayhap on this dim shore—
We shall meet to part no more."

Then the first Shade spoke and said :
"In this Kingdom of the Dead

6

" Let us, who so strangely meet,
Pledge each other in this sweet

" Water, our revenge to wreak
Side by side, and so to seek,

" Side by side, whate'er our fate,
Those we love and those we hate."

Kneeling on the dim shore then,
Side by side, they drank again.

And they saw, like drops of blood,
Poppies nodding o'er the flood,

And they gazed upon the thin
Ghostly web of mist, wherein

All things vague and changing seem
As the faces in a dream;

And by some enchantment weird,
As they gazed thereon appeared

Unto each, down-bending low,
Form and features of his foe,

7

For a moment, then were gone,
And upon the meadows wan—

Half in Death and half a-swoon—
Shone a pale and spectral moon.

Then these twain rose, drowsy-eyed,
And departed side by side.

But the Woman Shade the while
Smiled her cold, mysterious smile.

And her beauty made a light
In that realm of pallid night

(Beauty laughs at worm and grave)
Like the moon beneath the wave.

Back she flung her hair of gold,
Glowing, gleaming, fold on fold,

Showing—all but these might note—
The red ring around her throat.

But they passed with cold surprise,
And unrecognising eyes.

Lightly laughed she then, and said :
" In this Kingdom of the Dead

" Strange the sights that one may see !
There go twain who died for me

" Seeking, through Creation wide,
For each other—side by side !"

Then she wove a poppy crown,
Placed it on her head, and down

On the river's margin sank
Midst the poppies of its bank,

Saying : " In the world above
Long he tarries, my true love.

" Here beside this river's rim
I will sleep, and wait for him."

LOVE-LAUREL

AH! that God once would touch my lips with
    song
To pierce, as prayer doth heaven, earth's
    breast of iron,
    So that with sweet mouth I might sing to
    thee,
    O sweet dead singer buried by the sea,
A song, to woo thee, as a wooing siren,
Out of that silent sleep which seals too long
    Thy mouth of melody.

For, if live lips might speak awhile to dead,
Or any speech could reach the sad world under
    This world of ours, song surely should awake
    Thee who didst dwell in shadow for song's
    sake!

10

Alas! thou canst not hear the voice of thunder,
Nor low dirge over thy low-lying head
    The winds of morning make.

Down through the clay there comes no sound of
        these;
Down in the grave there is no sign of Summer,
    Nor any knowledge of the soft-eyed Spring;
    But Death sits there, with outspread ebon
        wing,
Closing with dust the mouth of each new-
        comer
To that mute land, where never sound of seas
    Is heard, and no birds sing.

Now thou hast found the end of all thy days
Hast thou found any heart a vigil keeping
    For thee among the dead—some heart that
        heard
    Thy singing when thou wert a brown, sweet
        bird

Gray æons gone, in some old forest sleeping
Beneath the seas long since? in Death's dim
ways
Has thy heart any word?

For surely those in whom the deathless spark
Of song is kindled, sang from the beginning
If life were always? But the old desires—
' Do they exist when sad-eyed Hope expires?
How live the dead? what crowns have they
for winning?
Have they, to warm them in the dreamless dark,
For sun earth's central fires?

Are the dead dead indeed whom we call dead?
Has God no life but this of ours for giving?—
When that they took thee by each well-
known place,
Stark in thy coffin with a cold white face,
What thought, O Brother, hadst thou of the
living?

What of the sun that round thee glory shed ?
What of the fair day's grace ?

Is thy new life made up of memories
Or dreams that lull the dead, bright visions
    bringing
Of Spring above ? Are thy days short or long?
Thou who wert master of our singing throng
Mayhap in death thou hast not lost thy singing,
But chauntst unheard, beside the moaning seas,
    A solitary song.

The chance spade turns up skulls.   God help the
    dead
And thee whose singing days have all passed
    over—
    Thee, whom the gold-haired spring shall
    seek in vain
    When at the glad year's doors she stands
    again,
Remembering the song—garlands thou hast
    wove her

In years gone by : but all these years have fled
  With all their joy and pain.

    .   .   .   .

My soul laughed out to hear my heart speak so,
And sprang forth skyward, as an eagle, hoping
  To look upon thy soul with living eyes,
  Until it came to where our dim life dies,
And dead suns darkly for a grave are groping
Through cycles of immeasurable woe,
  Stone-blind in the blind skies.

The stars walk shuddering on that awful verge
From which my soul, with swift and fearless
      motion,
  Clove the black depths, and sought for God
      and thee;
  But God dwells where nor stars nor suns
      there be—
No shore there is to His Eternal Ocean ;
A thousand systems are a fringe of surge
  On that great starless sea.

And thou wert not.   So that, with weary plumes,
My soul through the great void its way came
    winging
  To earth again.   "What hope for him who
    sings
  Is there?" it sighed.   "Death ends all sweetest
    things."
When lo! there came a swell of mighty singing,
Flooding all space, and swift athwart the gloom
  A flash of sudden wings.

        .   .   .   .

Dreamer of dreams, thy songs and dreams are
    done.
Down where thou sleepest in earth's secret
    bosom
  There is no sorrow and no joy for thee,
  Who canst not see what stars at eve there be,
Nor evermore at morn the green dawn blossom
Into the golden king-flower of the sun
  Across the golden sea.

But haply there shall come in days to be
One who shall hear his own heart beating
    faster,
  Plucking a rose sprung from thy heart be-
    neath,
  And from his soul, as sword from out its
    sheath,
Song shall leap forth where now, O silent
    master,
On thy lone grave beside the sounding sea,
  I lay this laurel-wreath.

A VISION OF YOUTH

A HORSEMAN on a hilltop green
  Drew rein, and wound his horn;
So bright he looked he might have been
  The Herald of the Morn.

His steed was of the sovran strain
  In Fancy's meadows bred—
And pride was in his tossing mane,
  And triumph in his tread.

The rider's eyes like jewels glowed—
  The World was in his hand—
As down the woodland way he rode
  When Spring was in the land.

From golden hour to golden hour
  For him the woodland sang,

And from the heart of every flower
A singing fairy sprang.

He rode along with rein so free,
And, as he rode, the Blue
Mysterious Bird of Fantasy
Ever before him flew.

He rode by cot and castle dim
Through all the greenland gay;
Bright eyes through casements glanced at
him;
He laughed—and rode away.

The world with sunshine was aflood,
And glad were maid and man,
And through his throbbing veins the blood
In keen, sweet shudders ran.

.   .   .   .

His steed tossed head with fiery scorn,
And stamped, and snuffed the air—
As though he heard a sudden horn
Of far-off battle blare.

Erect the rider sat awhile
  With flashing eyes, and then
Turned slowly, sighing, with a smile,
  " O weary world of men ! "

For aye the Bird of Fantasy
  Sang magic songs to him,
And deep and deeper still rode he
  Into the Forest Dim.

            .   .   .   .   .   .

That rider with his face aglow
  With joy of life I see
In dreams.   Ah, years and years ago
  He parted ways with me !

Yet, sometimes, when the days are drear
  And all the world forlorn,
From out the dim wood's heart I hear
  The echo of his horn.

APHRODITE

On a golden dawn in the dawn sublime
Of years ere the stars had ceased to sing,
Beautiful out of the sea-deeps cold
Aphrodite arose—the Flower of Time—
That, dear till the day of her blossoming,
The old, old Sea had borne in his heart.
Around her worshipping waves did part
Tremulous—glowing in rose and gold.

And the birds broke forth into singing sweet,
And flowers born scentless breathed perfume :
Softly she smiled upon Man forlorn,
And the music of love in his wild heart beat,
And down to the pit went his gods of gloom,
And earth grew bright and fair as a bride,
And folk in star-worlds wondering cried—
" Lo in the skies a new star is born !"

O Beloved, thus on my small world you
Rose, flushing it all with rosy flame!
Changing sad thoughts to a singing throng,
And creating the earth and the sky anew!
As Love you appeared—and, lo, you are Fame.
And, all my follies and sins despite,
You yet, Beloved, may see my light—
Small, but a star—mid the stars of song.

THE RAJAH'S SAPPHIRES

In my garden, O Beloved !
Many pleasant trees are growing,
Peach, and apricot, and apple,
Myrtle, lilac, and laburnum.

Fair are they, but midst them lonely,
Like an exiled Eastern Princess
In a strange land far from kindred,
Stands a lonely fair Pomegranate.

Dreaming of its native Orient
Always is the fair Pomegranate,
And beneath it I lie dreaming
Of thine eyes and thee, Beloved !

Overhead its red globes, gleaming
Like red moons, old tales recall of

Eastern moons and songs of Hafiz—
Nightingales, and wine, and roses.

And at times it seems a mystic
Tree Circéan, whose red fruit is
Broken hearts of old-time lovers,
Thus their secrets sad revealing.

And within each red sun-cloven
Glossy globe, like little rosy
Hearts within a great heart glowing,
Glow translucent seeds of crimson.

Like the fruit of the Pomegranate
Full of little hearts my heart is,
And the little hearts so glowing
They are thoughts of thee, Beloved!

Haply these at times are woven
In with dreams of the Pomegranate;
Thus, perchance, I dreamt the wondrous
Dream within a dream here written.

. . . . . .

In his palace-hall, methought, I
Saw a splendid Indian Rajah ;
Fame and Fortune were his vassals,
But his heart was sad within him.

Round him stood his chiefs and captains.
" Great art thou," they cried, " O Rajah !
And thy hand is strong in battle."
But he smiled not at their speeches.

Silently through his Zenana
Passed he, glanced with cold and careless
Eyes at women, fair as houris
Seen in visions bred of hasheesh.

Like to dawn, and noon, and starry
Night—like all the moods of passion—
Were they, rose-and-white Circassians,
Amber Hindoos, dark-eyed Persians.

Dancing girls with golden armlets,
Golden rings around their ankles—
Making music clear, melodious
As the plash of crystal fountains

Heard in still, hot nights of summer—
Danced the Lovers' Dance before him;
But he heeded not their dancing,
For his heart was sad within him.

Thence unto his treasure-chamber
Strode he—there to gaze on gems that
Rajahs dead had won and hoarded;
Tragic-storied, splendid jewels—

Flashing diamonds, like fallen
Stars, for whose bright evil beauty
Blood in old days had been spilt that
Should have made them burn like rubies;

Emeralds greener than Spring's garments,
Pearls like unto tears of Peris
Weeping by the gates of Eden;
Opals with their fateful lustre.

Long on these, and countless other
Many-coloured gems, the Rajah
Gazed, but found no more delight in
Their sun-flashing brilliant beauty.

He had dreamt a dream enchanting
Of twin-sapphires, blue as Heaven,
And his heart was filled with hunger
And with yearning to possess them.

Therefore unto his Vizier he
Told his dream, and gave command that
He should seek the wide world over,
Till he found the wondrous sapphires.

Doth that sad Vizier still wander
O'er the earth the sapphires seeking ?
Sooth, I know not—but I know that
He will never find them, never.

For they were no cold, bright sapphires
That the Rajah in his dream saw. . . .
Waking from my dream I knew that
They were thy blue eyes, Beloved !

THE CRUISE OF THE "IN MEMORIAM"

THE wan light of a stormy dawn
Gleamed on a tossing ship:
It was the *In Memoriam*
Upon a mourning trip.

Wild waves were on the windward bow,
And breakers on the lee;
And through her sides the women heard
The seething of the sea.

"O Captain!" cried a widow fair,
Her plump white hands clasped she,
"Thinkst thou, if drowned in this dread storm,
That savèd we shall be?"

"You speak in riddles, lady dear,
How savèd can we be

If we are drowned ?"   "Alas, I mean
  In Paradise !" said she.

" O I've sailed North, and I've sailed South "
  (He was a godless wight),
" But boy or man, since my days began,
  That shore I ne'er did sight !"

The Captain told the First Mate bold
  What that fair lady said ;
The First Mate sneered in his black
  beard—
  His eyes burned in his head.

" Full forty souls are here aboard,
  A-sailing on the wave—
Without the crew, and, 'twixt us two,
  I think *they've* none to save—

" Full forty souls, and each one is
  A mourner, as you know.
They weep the scuppers full ; the ship
  Is waterlogged with woe."

Again he sneered in his black beard :
" The cruise is not so brief,
But, ere we land on earthly strand,
  All will have found relief."

" Nay, nay," the Captain said, " First Mate,
  You have forgotten one
With eyes of blue; the tears are true
  From those dear eyes that run !

"She mourns her sweetheart drowned last year,
  A seaman *he*, forsooth !
I would not drown for Christ his crown
  If she were mine, Fair Ruth !"

" Brave words ! but words," the First Mate
    cried,
  " Are wind !   Behold in me
The warmest lover and the last !
  Mine shall the maiden be."

    .   .   .   .

Fair Ruth stood by the taffrail high,
  A cross dropped in the sea,

"If you lie here, my sweetheart dear,
  By this remember me!"

Fair Ruth stood by the taffrail high,
  A ring dropped in the sea:
"Marry him not, ye false mermaids,
  Married he's now to me!"

The heavens flashed flame; a black cloud
    came,
  Its wings the sky did span,
And hovered above the fated ship
  Like death o'er a dying man.

Bended the spars and shrieked the shrouds,
  The sails flew from the mast,
And, like a soul by fiends pursued,
  The ship fled through the blast.

"More sail! more sail!" the First Mate cried
  (The Captain stood aghast),
"More sail! more sail!" and he laughed in
    scorn,
  All by the mizen mast.

"O brethren dear, there's nought to fear,
  The steward told me so!"
'Twas the parson meek who thus did speak,
  Just come up from below :

"And *were* there," he said, with upraised head,
  And hands clasped piously,
"I have a sainted spouse in Heaven—
  I trow she waits for me."

Then grimly laughed the false First Mate :
  "Good parson, let her be !
I've a wife in every port but *that*—
  And that we shall not see."

"Oh, pardon seek !" cried the parson meek,
  "And pray, if pray you can,
For much I fear, by your scornful sneer,
  That you are a sinful man."

Then louder laughed the false First Mate,
  Louder and louder still,
And the wicked crew laughed loudly too,
  As wicked seamen will.

31

"O Captain!" whispered a gentle dame,
"When *shall* we see the land?"
The Captain answered never a word,
But clasped her by the hand.

. . . .

Day after day, night after night,
On, on the ship did reel:
The Captain drank with the second mate,
The First Mate held the wheel.

Down came a black cloud on the ship,
And wrapped her like a pall,
And horror of awful darkness fell
Upon them one and all.

The night had swallowed them utterly,
None could his fellow see,
But ghostly voices up and down
Went whispering fearsomely.

No faint ray shone from moon or sun,
The light of Heaven was gone,

But ever the First Mate held the wheel,
And ever the ship rushed on.

.   .   .   .

Fair Ruth knelt down in that grim gloom,
She prayed beneath her breath:
"God carry me o'er this dread sea
That seems the Sea of Death!"

She ceased—and lo! a lurid glow
O'er that dark water spread,
And in the blackness burned, afar,
A line of bloody red.

"What lights are yon?" the Captain said.
The First Mate answered then:
"No lights that ever shone upon
The world of living men."

"Down on your knees!" the parson cried;
"Thank God, for all is well!"
The First Mate laughed: "Those lights,
they are
The harbour lights of Hell."

c   33

On flew the ship; to every lip
  An ashen pallor came,
For all might see that suddenly
  The sea had turned to flame.

The lights were near; the Sea of Fear,
  Amid the silence dire,
On that dread shore broke evermore
  In soundless foam of fire.

" Oh, what are yon gray ghosts and wan ! "
  The parson cried, " who seem
With coloured strings of beads to play,
  As in a dreadful dream ?"

"Damned souls ;" the First Mate said ;
    " they sit
  And count, through endless years,
The moments of Eternity
  On beads of burning tears."

Then, " Who are you," the parson said,
  " That talk so free of Hell ?"

" My name is Satan," he replied,
" Have I not steered you well ?"

" Back—back the yards !" the Captain cried
Then quoth the false First Mate :
" Like many more who sight this shore,
You back your yards too late."

" There are the dear deceased you mourned
With such exceeding zest ;
They call you—whoso freely goes
E'en yet may save the rest."

One pale ghost waved the vessel back
With gestures sad and dumb—
Fair Ruth has plunged into the sea,
" My love, my love, I come !"

.   .   .   .

All in a moment shone the sun,
Blue gleamed the sky and sea,
The brave old ship upon the waves
Was dancing merrily.

And merrily to sound of bells
To her old port full soon
The *In Memoriam* that went forth
Returned the *Honeymoon*.

There o'er their grog sea-captains still
Her wondrous story tell,
And how her Captain backed his yards
A biscuit-throw from Hell.

IN A WINE CELLAR

SEE how it flashes,
  This grape-blood fine !—
Our beards it splashes,
  O comrade mine !—
Life dust and ashes
  Were, wanting wine.

Amontillado
  Fires heart and eyes;
Champagne the shadow
  Of care defies ;
An El Dorado
  In Rhine-wine lies;

Port has the mintage
  Of generous deeds ;

Tokay scorns stintage
And richly bleeds;
But this great vintage
The Wine-March leads.

Yet it is wanting
In poesy;
No legends haunting
Its vassals be,
No tales enchanting
Of chivalry.

Spain's grape hath stories;
Its blood the bold
Conquistadores
Drank deep of old—
A wine of glories,
A wine of gold.

Who drinks not sparing,
Beholdeth he
The great Cid bearing
His banner free,

Columbus daring
  The unknown Sea ;

And, haply biding,
  In this dream-Spain,
Don Quixote riding
  Across the plain,
His squire confiding
  Beside his rein.

The wine of France is
  Aglow to-day
With flash of lances,
  With feast and fray,
And dark-eyed glances
  Of ladies gay.

See where together,
  A flagon near,
Lie hat with feather,
  And long rapier—
Fine courting weather,
  O Cavalier !

39

Bright Rhenish, gleaming
  Moon-white! Perchance
Thy wave clear beaming
  Still guards Romance,
Not dead, but dreaming
  In spell-bound trance!

Not in Rhine-water,
  But Rhine-wine fair
Sir Rupert sought her
  (As bards declare)
The Rhine King's daughter
  With golden hair.

Still 'neath its smiling
  Wave's amber rings,
Men sweetly wiling
  From earthly things,
Her song beguiling
  The Loreley sings.

Your cup, wild siren,
  That Deutschland drains—

Her heart of iron
  Moved by your strains—
No blood shall fire in
  Australian veins;

Nor yours whose charm is
  Your topaz eyne,
Nor yours whose armies
  In gold caps shine,
Shall charm or harm us—
  Eh, comrade mine?

No vintage alien
  For thee or me!
Our fount Castalian
  Of poesy
Shall wine Australian,
  None other be.

Then place your hand in
  This hand of mine,
And while we stand in
  Her brave sunshine

Pledge deep our land in
Our land's own wine.

It has no glamour
Of old romance,
Of war and amour
In Spain or France ;
Its poets stammer
As yet, perchance ;

But he may wholly
Become a seer
Who quaffs it slowly ;
For he shall hear,
Though faintly, lowly,
Yet sweet and clear,

The axes ringing
On mountain sides,
The wool-boats swinging
Down Darling tides,
The drovers singing
Where Clancy rides,

The miners driving,
  The stockman's strife ;
All sounds conniving
  To tell the rife,
Rich, rude, strong-striving
  Australian life.

Once more your hand in
  This hand of mine !
And while we stand in
  The brave sunshine,
Pledge deep our land in
  Our land's own wine !

A-ROVING

When the sap runs up the tree,
  And the vine runs o'er the wall,
When the blossom draws the bee,
  From the forest comes a call,
Wild, and clear, and sweet, and strange,
  Many-toned and murmuring
Like the river in the range—
  'Tis the joyous voice of Spring!

On the boles of gray old trees
  See the flying sunbeams play
Mystic, soundless melodies—
  A fantastic march and gay;
But the young leaves hear them—hark,
  How they rustle, every one!—
And the sap beneath the bark
  Hearing, leaps to meet the sun.

44

O, the world is wondrous fair
  When the tide of life's at flood !
There is magic in the air,
  There is music in the blood ;
And a glamour draws us on
  To the Distance, rainbow-spanned,
And the road we tread upon
  Is the road to Fairyland.

Lo ! the elders hear the sweet
  Voice, and know the wondrous song ;
And their ancient pulses beat
  To a tune forgotten long ;
And they talk in whispers low,
  With a smile and with a sigh,
Of the years of long ago,
  And the roving days gone by.

BRUNETTE

When trees in Spring
Are blossoming
   My lady wakes
From dreams whose light
Made dark days bright,
   For their sweet sakes.

Yet in her eyes
A shadow lies
   Of bygone mirth;
And still she seems
To walk in dreams,
   And not on earth.

46

Some men may hold
That hair of gold
  Is lovelier
Than darker sheen :
They have not seen
  My lady's hair.

Her eyes are bright,
Her bosom white
  As the sea foam
On sharp rocks sprayed ;
Her mouth is made
  Of honeycomb.

And whoso seeks
In her dusk cheeks
  May see Love's sign—
A blush that glows
Like a red rose
  Beneath brown wine.

YEARS AGO

THE old dead flowers of bygone summers,
  The old sweet songs that are no more sung,
The rose-red dawns that were welcome comers
  When you and I and the world were young,

Are lost, O love, to the light for ever,
  And seen no more of the moon or sun,
For seas divide, and the seasons sever,
  And twain are we that of old were one.

O fair lost love, when the ship went sailing
  Across the seas in the years agone,
And seaward-set were the eyes unquailing,
  And landward-looking the faces wan,

My heart went back as a dove goes homeward
  With wings aweary to seek its nest,

While fierce sea-eagles are flying foamward
  And storm-winds whiten the surge's crest;

And far inland for a farewell pardon
  Flew on and on, while the ship went South—
The rose was red in the red-rose garden,
  And red the rose of your laughing mouth.

But no word came on the wind in token
  Of love that lasts till the end; and so
My heart returned to me bruised and broken,
  From you, my love, of the long ago.

The green fields seemed in the distance growing
  To silken squares on a weaver's loom,
As oversea came the land-wind blowing
  The faint sweet scent of the clover bloom.

A rarer odour to me it carried,
  In subtle delicate way to tell
Of you, ere you and the world were married—
  The lilac-odour you loved so well.

D   49

Again, I saw you beneath the blooms of
   Those lilac-trees in the garden old.
Ah me! each tree is a mark for tombs of
   Dead dreams and memories still and cold.

And Death comes there with his breath scent-
      laden,
   And gathering gently the blossoms shed
(In guise of Autumn, the brown-browed maiden)
   With your and my dead buries his dead.

O, fairer far than the fair ideal
   Of him who imaged the foam-born Queen
In foam-white marble—a dream made real—
   To me were you in those years, I ween.

Your lips were redder than night-shade berries
   That burn in borders of hedgerowed lanes,
And sweeter far than the sweet wild cherries
   The June sun flushes with crimson stains.

And gray your eyes as a gray dove's wings were—
   A gray soft-shadowing deeps profound,

Where thoughts that reached to the heart of
    things were,
And love lay dreaming though seeming
    drowned.

Twin-tulip-breasted like her the tread of
    Whose feet made music in Paphos fair,
The world to me was not worth a thread of
    Your brown, ambrosial, braided hair.

Mayhap you loved me at one time truly,
    And I was jealous, and you were proud;
But mine the love of the king in Thule,
    Till death; and yours—sleeps well in shroud.

So night came down like a sombre raven,
    And southward ever the ship was borne,
Till glad green fields and lessening haven
    Grew faint and faded like ghosts at morn.

As fields of Heaven eternal blooming,
    Those flowerful fields of my mother-land
In midnight visions are still perfuming
    All wild waste places and seas of sand.

And still in seasons of storm and thunder,
  In strange lands under your land and mine,
And though our ways have been wide asunder,
  In calm and tempest and shade and shine

Your face I see as I saw the last time—
  As one borne space-ward on wings of light,
With eyes turned back to a sight of past time,
  Beholds for ever that self-same sight.

But scorn has died on your lips, and through you
  Shines out star-bright an immortal grace,
As though God then to His heaven drew you,
  And sent an angel to take your place.

I plucked one rose from the tree you cherished,
  My heart's blood ebbing has kept it red,
And all my hopes with its scent have perished;
  Why mourn them now—are the dead not dead?

And yet, God knows, as this rose I kiss, you
  May feel the kisses across the sea;
And soul to soul for the larger issue
  Your soul may stand with the soul of me,

Unknown to you—for the strings of Being
    Are not so easily snapped or torn ;
And we may journey with eyes unseeing
    On paths that meet in the years unborn.

Farewell, dear heart.   Warm sighs may sever
    Ripe lips of love like a rose-leaf curled,
But you remain unto me for ever
    The one fair woman in all the world.

VILLANELLE

WE said farewell, my youth and I,
    When all fair dreams were gone or going,
And Love's red lips were cold and dry.

When white blooms fell from tree-tops high—
    Our Austral winter's way of snowing—
We said farewell, my youth and I.

We did not sigh—what use to sigh
    When Death passed as a mower mowing,
And Love's red lips were cold and dry ?

But hearing Life's stream thunder by,
    That sang of old through flowers flowing,
We said farewell, my youth and I.

There was no hope in the blue sky,
  No music in the low winds blowing,
And Love's red lips were cold and dry.

My hair is black as yet, then why
  So sad! I know not, only knowing
We said farewell, my youth and I.

All are not buried when they die;
  Dead souls there are through live eyes showing
When Love's red lips are cold and dry.

So, seeing where the dead men lie,
  Out of their hearts the grave-flowers growing,
We said farewell, my youth and I,
When Love's red lips were cold and dry.

THE VOICE OF THE SOUL

In Youth, when through our veins runs fast
  The bright red stream of life,
The Soul's Voice is a trumpet-blast
  That calls us to the strife.

The Spirit spurns its prison-bars,
  And feels with force endued
To scale the ramparts of the stars
  And storm Infinitude.

Youth passes ; like a dungeon grows
  The Spirit's house of clay :
The voice that once in music rose
  In murmurs dies away.

But in the day when sickness sore
  Smites on the body's walls,

The Soul's Voice through the breach once more
  Like to a trumpet calls.

Well shall it be with him who heeds
  The mystic summons then !
His after-life with loving deeds
  Shall blossom amongst men.

He shall have gifts—the gift that feels
  The germ within the clod,
And hears the whirring of the wheels
  That turn the mills of God !

The gift that sees with glance profound
  The secret soul of things,
And in the silence hears the sound
  Of vast and viewless wings !

The veil of Isis sevenfold
  To him as gauze shall be,
Wherethrough, clear-eyed, he shall behold
  The Ancient Mystery.

He shall do battle for the True,
  Defend till death the Right,
With Shoes of Swiftness Wrong pursue,
  With Sword of Sharpness smite.

And, dying, he shall haply hear,
  Like golden trumpets blown
For joy, far voices sweet and clear—
  Soul-voices like his own.

So welcomed may he join the Throng
  Upon the Shining Shore,
As one who, after wandering long,
  Returneth home once more!

CARES

Having certain cares to drown,
To the sea I took them down :

And I threw them in the wave,
That engulfed them like a grave.

Swiftly then I plied the oar
With a light heart to the shore.

But behind me came my foes :
Like a nine-days' corpse each rose,

And (a ghastly sight to see !)
Clutched the boat and girned at me !

With a heavy heart, alack,
To the land I bore them back.

Not in Water or in Wine
Can I drown these cares of mine.

But some day, for good and sure,
I shall bury them secure,

Where the soil is rich and brown,
With a stone to keep them down,

And to let their end be known,
Have my name carved on the stone ;

So that passers-by may say,
" Here lie cares that had their day,"

And sometimes by moonlight wan,
I may sit that stone upon—

With a spectre's solemn phlegm—
In my shroud, and laugh at them ;

Or—who knows, when all is said ?—
Maybe weep because they're dead.

PONCÉ DE LÉON

By a black wharf I stood lately,
  When the night was at its noon;
Keen, malicious stars were shining,
  And a wicked, white-faced moon.

And I saw a stately vessel,
  Built in fashion quaint and old;
From her masthead, in the moonlight,
  Hung a flag of faded gold.

Black with age her masts and spars were,
  Black with age her ropes and rails;
Like a ghost through cere-cloths gazing
  Shone the white moon through her sails.

Not a movement stirred the stillness,
  Not a sound the silence broke,

Save alone the livid water
    Lapping round her sides of oak.

Then to her unseen commander
    Spake I, as to one I knew—
"Don Juan Poncé de Léon,
    I have waited long for you.

"Take me with you, I implore you!
    Take me with you on your quest
For the Fount of Youth Eternal,
    For the Islands of the Blest."

Then above the bulwarks ancient
    I beheld a head arise;
And the moon with ghastly glimmer
    Lit its sad and hollow eyes.

"Grieved am I, señor, and sorry,"
    Very courteously it said,
"That I may not take you with me—
    But I only take the Dead.

"These alone may dare the voyage,
　　These alone sail on the quest
For the Fount of Youth Eternal,
　　For the Islands of the Blest."

DEATH

THE awful seers of old, who wrote in words
  Like drops of blood great thoughts that
    through the night
Of ages burn, as eyes of lions light
Deep jungle-dusks; who smote with songs like
  swords
The soul of man on its most secret chords,
  And made the heart of him a harp to smite,—
  Where are they? where that old man lorn of
    sight,
The king of song among these laurelled lords?
But where are all the ancient singing-spheres
  That burst through chaos like the summer's
    breath
Through ice-bound seas where never seaman
    steers?
Burnt out. Gone down. No star remembereth
These stars and seers well-silenced through the
    years—
  The songless years of everlasting death.

LIFE

WHAT know we of the dead, who say these things,
  Or of the life in death below the mould—
What of the mystic laws that rule the old
Gray realms beyond our poor imaginings
Where death is life ?   The bird with spray-wet
    wings
    Knows more of what the deeps beneath him
    hold.
  Let be : warm hearts shall never wax a-cold,
But burn in roses through eternal springs :
For all the vanished fruit and flower of Time
  Are flower and fruit in worlds we cannot see,
And all we see is as a shadow-mime
  Of things unseen, and Time that comes to flee
Is but the broken echo of a rhyme
  In God's great epic of Eternity.

CHRISTMAS IN AUSTRALIA

O DAY, the crown and crest of all the year !
Thou comest not to us amid the snows,
But midmost of the reign of the red rose ;
Our hearts have not yet lost the ancient cheer
That filled our fathers' simple hearts when sere
The leaves fell, and the winds of Winter froze
The waters wan, and carols at the close
Of yester-eve sang the Child Christ anear.
And so we hail thee with a greeting high,
And drain to thee a draught of our own wine,
Forgetful not beneath this bluer sky
Of that old mother-land beyond the brine,
Whose gray skies gladden as thou drawest nigh,
O day of God's good-will the seal and sign !

QUESTIONS

Soul, dost thou shudder at the narrow tomb?
    Heart, dost thou dread to moulder in the dust—
    To meet the fate that all things mortal must,
Strength in its pride, and beauty in its bloom?
What have ye done to merit nobler doom?
    How used one life that ye for more should lust?
    Time in his course doth all things downward
        thrust:
The unborn generations wait for room!
Blind we were born, blind die: yet we must still
    Take God to task with Whither? Whence?
        and Why?
What if God, giving us our wish and will,
    Said, "Judge thyself" to each! Who dares
        reply?
He knows the end who made the perfect plan—
Hell were too small if man were judged by man.

THE GODS

Last night, as one who hears a tragic jest,
  I woke from dreams, half-laughing, half in
    tears;
Methought that I had journeyed in the spheres
And stood upon the Planet of the Blest!
And found thereon a folk who prayed with zest
  Exceeding, and through all their painful years,
  Like strong souls struggled on, 'mid hopes and
    fears;
"Where dwell the gods," they said, "we shall
    find rest."
The gods? What gods, I thought, are these who so
  Inspire their worshippers with faith that flowers
Immortal, and who make them keep aglow
  The flames for ever on their altar-towers?
"Where dwell these gods of yours?" I asked—
    and lo!
  They pointed upward to this earth of ours!

THE GLEANER

METHOUGHT I came unto a world-wide plain
  Where souls stood thick as grain at harvest-
    tide,
  And many reapers, full of pious pride,
With rapid scythe-sweeps mowed them down
    amain;
And zealous binders bound them up like grain
  In sheaves: the reapers at each onward stride
  Trod many souls down. These the binders
    eyed
With careless looks or glances of disdain.
But, following slow, a patient Gleaner came
  And gathered all the Binders cast aside,
  And made fair sheaves thereof. Whereat I
    cried:
" Why gather these? Who art thou? Name thy
    name!"
  The Gleaner in a sad, sweet voice replied:
" The outcasts' Saviour—for these, too, I died."

LOVE

Love is the sunlight of the soul,
That, shining on the silken-tressèd head
Of her we love, around it seems to shed
  A golden angel-aureole.

And all her ways seem sweeter ways
Than those of other women in that light :
She has no portion with the pallid night,
  But is a part of all fair days.

Joy goes where she goes, and good dreams—
Her smile is tender as an old romance
Of Love that dies not, and her soft eye's glance
  Like sunshine set to music seems.

Queen of our fate is she, but crowned
With purple hearts-ease for her womanhood.

There is no place so poor where she has stood
But evermore is holy ground.

An angel from the heaven above
Would not be fair to us as she is fair:
She holds us in a mesh of silken hair,
    This one sweet woman whom we love.

We pray thee, Love, our souls to steep
In dreams wherein thy myrtle flowereth;
So when the rose leaves shiver, feeling Death
    Pass by, we may remain asleep:

Asleep, with poppies in our hands,
From all the world and all its cares apart—
Cheek close to cheek, heart beating against heart,
    While through Life's sandglass run the sands.

PASSION FLOWER

Choose who will the wiser part—
I have held her heart to heart;

And have felt her heart-strings stirred,
And her soul's still singing heard

For one golden-haloed hour
Of Love's life the passion-flower.

So the world may roll or rest—
I have tasted of its best;

And shall laugh while I have breath
At thy dart and thee, O Death!

TO MY LADY

WHEN the tender hand of Night
　Like a rose-leaf falls
Softly on your starry eyes;
　When the Sleep-God calls,
And the gate of dreams is wide,
　Wide the painted halls,
Dream the dream I send to you
　Through your spirit's walls!

Dream a lowly lover came,
　Lady fair to woo;
Dream that I the lover was,
　And the lady—you;
Dream your answer was a kiss,
　Warm as summer dew—
Waking, in the rosy dawn,
　Let the dream be true!

73

THE HAWTHORN

By the road, near her father's dwelling,
  There groweth a hawthorn tree :
Its blossoms are fair and fragrant
  As the love that I cast from me.

It is all a-bloom this morning
  In the sunny silentness,
And grows by the roadside, radiant
  As a bride in her bridal dress.

But ah me ! at sight of its blossoms
  No pleasant memories start :
I see but the thorns beneath them—
  And the thorns they pierce my heart.

SPRING DIRGE

A CHILD came singing through the dusty town
    A song so sweet that all men stayed to hear,
    Forgetting for a space their ancient fear
Of evil days and death and fortune's frown.

She sang of Winter dead and Spring new-born
    In the green fields beyond the far hills' bound;
    And how this fair Spring, coming blossom-
        crowned,
Would cross the city's threshold on the morn.

And each caged bird in every house anigh,
    Even as she sang, caught up the glad refrain
    Of Love and Hope and fair days come again,
Till all who heard forgot they had to die.

And all the ghosts of buried woes were laid
    That heard the song of this sweet sorceress;
    The Past grew to a dream of old distress,
And merry were the hearts of man and maid.

So, at the first faint blush of tender dawn,
    Spring stole with noiseless steps through the
        gray gloom,
    And men knew only by a strange perfume
That she had softly entered and withdrawn.

But ah! the lustre of her violet eyes
    Was dimmed with tears for her sweet singing
        maid,
    Whose voice would sound no more in shine or
        shade
To charm men's souls at set of sun or rise.

For there, with dews of dawn upon her hair,
    Like a fair flower plucked and flung away,
    Dead in the street the little maiden lay
Who gave new life to hearts nigh dead of care.

Alas! must this be still the bitter doom
Awaiting those, the finer-souled of earth,
Who make for men a morning song of mirth
While yet the birds are dumb amid the gloom ?

They walk on thorny ways with feet unshod,
Sing one last song, and die as that song dies.
There is no human hand to close their eyes,
And very heavy is the hand of God.

FRAGMENTS

These broken lines for pardon crave ;
I cannot end the song with art :
My grief is gray and old—her grave
Is dug so deep within my heart.

I.—HER LAST DAY

IT was a day of sombre heat :
The still, dense air was void of sound
And life ; no wing of bird did beat
A little breeze through it—the ground
Was like live ashes to the feet.
From the black hills that loomed around
The valley many a sudden spire
Of flame shot up, and writhed, and curled,
And sank again for heaviness :

And heavy seemed to men that day
The burden of the weary world.
For evermore the sky did press
Closer upon the earth that lay
Fainting beneath, as one in dire
Dreams of the night, upon whose breast
Sits a black phantom of unrest
That holds him down. The earth and sky
Appeared unto the troubled eye
A roof of smoke, a floor of fire.

There was no water in the land.
Deep in the night of each ravine
Men, vainly searching for it, found
Dry hollows in the gaping ground,
Like sockets where clear eyes had been,
Now burnt out with a burning brand.
There was no water in the land
But the salt sea tide, that did roll
Far past the places where, till then,
The sweet streams met and flung it back ;
The beds of little brooks, that stole

In spring-time down each ferny glen,
And rippled over rock and sand,
Were drier than a cattle-track.
A dull, strange languor of disease,
That ever with the heat increased,
Fell upon man, and bird, and beast ;
The thin-flanked cattle gasped for breath ;
The birds dropped dead from drooping trees ;
And men, who drank the muddy lees
From each near-dry though deep-dug well,
Grew faint ; and over all things fell
A heavy stupor, dank as Death.

. . . .

Fierce Nature, glaring with a face
Of savage scorn at my despair,
Withered my heart. From cone to base
The hills were full of hollow eyes
That rayed out darkness, dead and dull ;
Gray rocks grinned under ridges bare,
Like dry teeth in a mouldered skull ;
And ghastly gum-tree trunks did loom

Out of black clefts and rifts of gloom,
As sheeted spectres that arise
From yawning graves at dead of night
To fill the living with affright;
And, like to witches foul that bare
Their withered arms, and bend, and cast
Dread curses on the sleeping lands
In awful legends of the past,
Red gums, with outstretched bloody hands,
Shook maledictions in the air.

Fear was around me everywhere :
The wrinkled foreheads of the rocks
Frowned on me, and methought I saw—
Deep down in dismal gulfs of awe,
Where   gray   death - adders   have   their
     lair,
With the fiend-bat, the flying-fox,
And dim sun-rays, down-groping far,
Pale as a dead man's fingers are—
The grisly image of Decay,
That at the root of Life doth gnaw.

Sitting alone upon a throne
Of rotting skull and bleaching bone.

.   .   .   .
.

"There is an end to all our griefs :
Little the red worm of the grave
Will vex us when our days are done."
So changed my thought : up-gazing then
On gray-piled stones that seemed the cairns
Of dead and long-forgotten chiefs—
The men of old, the poor wild men
Who, under dim lights, fought a brave,
Sad fight of Life, where hope was none,
In the vague, voiceless, far-off years—
It changed again to present pain,
And I saw Sorrow everywhere :
In blackened trees and rust-red ferns,
Blasted by bush-fires and the sun ;
And by the salt-flood—salt as tears—
Where the wild apple-trees hung low,
And evermore stooped down to stare
At their drowned shadows in the wave,

Wringing their knotted hands of woe ;
And the dark swamp-oaks, row on row,
Lined either bank—a sombre train
Of mourners with down-streaming hair.

II.—SUNSET

THE day and its delights are done ;
  So all delights and days expire :
Down in the dim, sad West the sun
  Is dying like a dying fire.

The fiercest lances of his light
  Are spent ; I watch him droop and die
Like a great king who falls in fight ;
  None dared the duel of his eye
Living, but, now his eye is dim,
The eyes of all may stare at him.

How lovely in his strength at morn
He orbed along the burning blue !
The blown gold of his flying hair
Was tangled in green-tressèd trees,

83

And netted in the river sand
In gleaming links of amber clear;
But all his shining locks are shorn,
His brow of its bright crown is bare,
The golden sceptre leaves his hand,
And deeper, darker, grows the hue
Of the dim purple draperies
And cloudy banners round his bier.

O beautiful, rose-hearted dawn !—
O splendid noon of gold and blue !—
Is this wan glimmer all of you ?
Where are the blush and bloom ye gave
To laughing land and smiling sea ?—
The swift lights that did flash and shiver
In diamond rain upon the river,
And set a star in each blue wave ?
Where are the merry lights and shadows
That danced through wood and over lawn,
And flew across the dewy meadows
Like white nymphs chased by satyr lovers ?
Faded and perished utterly.

All delicate and all rich colour
In flower and cloud, on lawn and lea,
On butterfly, and bird, and bee,
A little space and all are gone—
And darkness, like a raven, hovers
Above the death-bed of the day.

.   .   .   .   .   .

So, when the long, last night draws on,
And all the world grows ghastly gray,
We see our beautiful and brave
Wither, and watch with heavy sighs
The life-light dying in their eyes,
The love-light slowly fading out,
Leaving no faint hope in their place,
But only on each dear wan face
The shadow of a weary doubt,
The ashen pallor of the grave.

O gracious morn and golden noon !
With what fair dreams did ye depart—
Beloved so well and lost so soon !

I could not fold you to my breast :
I could not hide you in my heart ;
I saw the watchers in the West—
Sad, shrouded shapes, with hands that wring
And phantom fingers beckoning !

III.—YEARS AFTER

Fade off the ridges, rosy light,
Fade slowly from the last gray height,
And leave no gloomy cloud to grieve
The heart of this enchanted eve !

All things beneath the still sky seem
Bound by the spell of a sweet dream ;
In the dusk forest, dreamingly,
Droops slowly down each plumèd head ;
The river flowing softly by
Dreams of the sea ; the quiet sea
Dreams of the unseen stars ; and I
Am dreaming of the dreamless dead.

The river has a silken sheen,
But red rays of the sunset stain

Its pictures, from the steep shore caught,
Till shades of rock, and fern, and tree
Glow like the figures on a pane
Of some old church by twilight seen,
Or like the rich devices wrought
In mediæval tapestry.

All lonely in a drifting boat
Through shine and shade I float and float,
Dreaming and dreaming, till I seem
Part of the picture and the dream.

There is no sound to break the spell,
No voice of bird or stir of bough ;
Only the lisp of waters wreathing
In little ripples round the prow,
And a low air, like Silence breathing,
That hardly dusks the sleepy swell
Whereon I float to that strange deep
That sighs upon the shores of Sleep.

.   .   .   .   .   .

But in the silent heaven blooming
　　Behold the wondrous sunset flower
　　That blooms and fades within the hour—
The flower of fantasy, perfuming
　　With subtle melody of scent
　　The blue aisles of the firmament!

For colour, music, scent, are one;
　　From deeps of air to airless heights,
Lo! how he sweeps, the splendid sun,
　　His burning lyre of many lights!

See the clear golden lily blowing!
　　It shines as shone thy gentle soul,
　　O my most sweet, when from the goal
　　Of life, far-gazing, thou didst see—
　　While Death still feared to touch thine eyes,
Where such immortal light was glowing—
　　The vision of eternity,
　　The pearly gates of Paradise!

Now richer hues the skies illume:
The pale gold blushes into bloom,　.

Delicate as the flowering
Of first love in the tender spring
Of Life, when love is wizardry
   That over narrow days can throw
   A glamour and a glory ! so
Did thine, my Beautiful, for me
   So long ago ; so long ago.

So long ago ! so long ago !
   Ah, who can Love and Grief estrange ?
Or Memory and Sorrow part ?
   Lo, in the West another change—
   A deeper glow : a rose of fire :
   A rose of passionate desire
Lone burning in a lonely heart.

A lonely heart ; a lonely flood.
The wave that glassed her gleaming head
And smiling passed, it does not know
That gleaming head lies dark and low ;
The myrtle-tree that bends above,
I pray that it may early bud,
For under its green boughs sat we—

We twain, we only, hand in hand,
When Love was lord of all the land—
It does not know that she is dead
And all is over now with Love,
Is over now with Love and me.

Once more, once more, O shining years
Gone by; once more, O vanished days
Whose hours flew by on iris-wings,
Come back and bring my love to me!
My voice faints down the wooded ways
And dies along the darkling flood.
The past is past; I cry in vain,
For when did Death an answer deign
To Love's heart-broken questionings?
The dead are deaf; dust chokes their ears;
Only the rolling river hears
Far off the calling of the sea—
A shiver strikes through all my blood,
Mine eyes are full of sudden tears.

.   .   .   .   .   .

The shadows gather over all,
  The valley, and the mountains old;
Shadow on shadow fast they fall
  On glooming green and waning gold;
And on my heart they gather drear,
Damp as with grave-damps, dark with fear.

.   .   .   .

O Sorrow, Sorrow, couldst thou leave me
  Not one brief hour to dream alone?
Hast thou not all my days to grieve me?
  My nights, are they not all thine own?
Thou hauntest me at morning light,
  Thou blackenest the white moonbeams;
A hollow voice at noon; at night
  A crowned ghost, sitting on a throne,
  Ruling the kingdom of my dreams.

.   .   .   .

Maker of men, Thou gavest breath,
Thou gavest love to all that live,
Thou rendest loves and lives apart;

91

Allwise art Thou; who questioneth
Thy will, or who can read Thy heart?
But couldst Thou not in mercy give
A sign to us—one little spark
Of sure hope that the end of all
Is not concealed beneath the pall,
Or wound up with the winding-sheet?
Who heedeth aught the preacher saith
When eyes wax dim, and limbs grow stark,
And fear sits on the darkened bed?
The dying man turns to the wall.
What hope have we above our dead?—
Tense fingers clutching at the dark,
And hopeless hands that vainly beat
Against the iron doors of Death!

"UNTO THIS LAST"

THEY brought my fair love out upon a bier—
Out from the dwelling that her smile made
     sweet,
Out from the life that her life made complete,
Into the glitter of the garish street—
And no man wept, save I, for that dead dear.

And then the dark procession wound along,
Like a black serpent with a snow-white bird
Held in its fangs.   I think God said a word
To death, as He in His chill heaven heard
Her voice so sweeter than His seraph's song.

And so Death took away her flower-sweet breath
One darkest day of days in a dark year, [dear
And brought to that strong God who had no
My own dear love.   Ah, closed eyes without
     a peer !
Ah, red lips pressed on the blue lips of Death !

93

THE NIGHTINGALE

WHEN the moon a golden-pale
  Lustre on my casement flings,
An enchanted nightingale
  In the haunted silence sings.

Strange the song—its wondrous words
  Taken from the primal tongue,
Known to men, and beasts, and birds,
  When the care-worn world was young.

Listening low, I hear the stars
  Through her strains move solemnly,
And on lonesome banks and bars
  Hear the sobbing of the sea.

And my memory dimly gropes
  Hints to gather from her song

94

Of forgotten fears and hopes,
  Joys and griefs forgotten long.

And I feel once more the strife
  Of a passion, fierce and grand,
That, in some long-vanished life,
  Held my soul at its command.

Ah, my Love, in robes of white
  Standing by a moonlit sea,
Like a lily of the night,
  Hast thou quite forgotten me ?

Dost thou never dream at whiles
  Of that silent, templed vale,
And the dim wood in whose aisles
  Sang a secret nightingale ?

Whither hast thou gone ?   What star
  Holds thy spirit pure and fine ?
In this world below there are
  None like thee : and thou wert mine !

For a season all things last,
　Love and Joy, and Life and Death ;
Thou art portion of my past,
　I of thine, whilst Time draws breath.

Fades the moonlight golden-pale,
　And the bird has ceased to sing—
Ah, it was no nightingale,
　But my heart—remembering.

THE TWO KEYS

Thᴇʀᴇ was a Boy, long years ago,
  Who hour by hour awake would lie,
And watch the white moon gliding slow
  Along her pathway in the sky.

And every night as thus he lay
  Entranced in lonely fantasy,
Borne swiftly on a bright moon-ray
  There came to him a Golden Key.

And with that Golden Key the Boy
  Oped every night a magic door
That to a melody of Joy
  Turned on its hinges evermore.

Then, trembling with delight and awe,
  When he the charmèd threshold crossed,
A radiant corridor he saw—
  Its end in dazzling distance lost.

Great windows shining in a row
  Lit up the wondrous corridor,
And each its own rich light did throw
  In stream resplendent on the floor.

One window showed the Boy a scene
  Within a forest old and dim,
Where fairies danced upon the green
  And kissed their little hands to him.

Sweet strains of elfin harp and horn
  He heard so clearly sounding there,
And he to Wonderland was borne
  And breathed its soft enchanted air.

Then, passing onward with the years,
  He turned his back on Elf and Fay,
And sadly sweet, as if in tears,
  The fairy music died away.

The second window held him long :
  It looked upon a field of fight
Whereon the countless hordes of Wrong
  Fought fiercely with the friends of Right.

And, lo ! upon that fateful field,
  Where cannon thundered, banners streamed,
And rushing squadrons rocked and reeled,
  His sword a star of battle gleamed.

And when the hordes of Wrong lay still,
  And that great fight was fought and won,
He stood, bright-eyed, upon a hill,
  His white plume shining in the sun.

A glorious vision ! yet behind
  He left it with its scarlet glow,
And faint and far upon the wind
  He heard the martial trumpets blow.

For to his listening ear was borne
  A music more entrancing far
Than strains of elfin harp or horn,
  More thrilling than the trump of war.

99

No longer as a dreamy boy
    He trod the radiant corridor :
His young man's heart presaged a joy
    More dear than all the joys of yore.

To that third window, half in awe,
    He moved, and slowly raised his eyes—
And was it earth grown young he saw ?
    Or was it man's lost Paradise ?

For all the flowers that ever bloomed
    Upon the earth, and all the rare
Sweet Loveliness by Time entombed,
    Seemed blushing, blooming, glowing there.

And every mellow-throated bird
    That ever sang the trees among
Seemed singing there, with one sweet word—
    "Love ! Love !" on every little tongue.

Then he by turns grew rosy-red,
    And he by turns grew passion-pale.
" Sweet Love !" the lark sang overhead,
    " Sweet Love !" sang Love's own nightingale.

In mid-heart of the hawthorn-tree
  The thrush sang all its buds to bloom;
"Love! Love! Love! Love! Sweet Love," sang
    he
  Amidst the soft green sun-flecked gloom.

            .   .   .   .

She stood upon a lilied lawn,
  With dreamful eyes that gazed afar:
A maiden tender as the Dawn
  And lovely as the Morning Star.

She stooped and kissed him on the brow,
  And in a low, sweet voice said she:
"I am this country's queen—and thou?"
  "I am thy vassal," murmured he.

She hid him with her hair gold-red,
  That flowed like sunshine to her knee;
She kissed him on the lips, and said:
  "Dear heart! I've waited long for thee."

And, oh, she was so fair, so fair,
  So gracious was her beauty bright,
Around her the enamoured air
  Pulsed tremulously with delight.

In passionate melody did melt
  Bird-voices, scent of flower and tree,
And he within his bosom felt
  The piercing thorn of ecstasy.

          .   .   .   .   .   .

The years passed by in dark and light,
  In storm and shine; the man grew old,
Yet never more by day or night
  There came to him the Key of Gold.

But ever, ere the great sun flowers
  In gold above the sky's blue rim,
All in the dark and lonely hours
  There comes an Iron Key to him.

And with that key he opes a wide
  And gloomy door—the Door of Fate—

That makes, whene'er it swings aside,
  A music sad and desolate,

A music sad from saddest source :
  He sees beside the doorway set
The chill, gray figure of Remorse,
  The pale, cold image of Regret.

For all the glory and the glow
  Of Life are passed, and dead, and gone :
The Light and Life of Long Ago
  Are memories only moonlight-wan.

        .   .   .   .   .   .

There is no man of woman born
  So brave, so good, so wise but he
Must sometimes in a night forlorn
  Take up and use the Iron Key.

LACHESIS

Over a slow-dying fire,
  Dreaming old dreams, I am sitting;
The flames leap up and expire;
  A woman sits opposite knitting.

I've taken a Fate to wife;
  She knits with a half-smile mocking
Me, and my dreams, and my life,
  All into a worsted stocking.

SYMBOLS

'Tis said that the Passion Flower,
  With its figures of spear and sword
And hammer and nails, is a symbol
  Of the Woe of our Blessed Lord.

So still in the Heart of Beauty
  Has been hidden, since Life drew breath,
The sword and the spear of Anguish,
  And the hammer and nails of Death.

AT THE OPERA

THE curtain rose—the play began—
    The limelight on the gay garbs shone ;
    Yet carelessly I gazed upon
The painted players, maid and man,
      As one with idle eyes who sees
      The marble figures on a frieze.

Long lark-notes clear the first act close,
    So the soprano : then a hush—
    The tenor, tender as a thrush ;
Then loud and high the chorus rose,
      Till, with a sudden rush and strong,
      It ended in a storm of song.

The curtain fell—the music died—
    The lights grew bright, revealing there
    The flash of jewelled fingers fair,

And wreaths of pearls on brows of pride ;
   Then, with a quick-flushed cheek, I turned,
   And into mine her dark eyes burned.

Such eyes but once a man may see,
   And, seeing once, his fancy dies
   To thought of any other eyes :
So shadow-soft, they seemed to be
   Twin haunted lakes, lit by the gleams
   Of a mysterious moon of dreams.

Silk lashes veiled their liquid light
   With such a shade as tall reeds fling
   From the lake-marge at sunsetting :
Their darkness might have hid the night—
   Yet whoso saw their glance would say
   Night dreamt therein, and saw the day.

Long looked I at them, wondering
   What tender memories were hid
   Beneath each blue-veined lily-lid ;
What hopes of joys the years would bring ;
   What griefs ? In vain : I might not guess
   The secret of their silentness.

What of her face ?   Her face, meseems,
   Was such as painters see who muse
   By moonlight in dim avenues,
Yet cannot paint; or as in dreams,
   Young poets see, but, when they try
   To limn in verse are dumb—so I.

Yet well I know that I have seen
   That sweet face in tho long ago
   In a rose-bower—well I know—
Laughing the singing leaves between,
   In that strange land of rose and rhyme—
   The land of Once upon a Time.

O unknown sweet, so sweetly known,
   I know not what your name may be—
   Madonna is your name for me—
Nor where your lines in life are thrown;
   But soul sees soul—what is the rest ?
   A passing phantom at the best.

Did your young bosom never glow
   To love ? or burns your heart beneath
   As burns the rosebud in its sheath ?

I neither know nor wish to know :
  I smell the rose upon the tree ;
  Who will may pluck and wear, for me—

May wear the rose, and watch it die,
  And, leaf by red leaf, fade and fall,
  Till there be nothing left at all
Of its sweet loveliness ; but I
  Love it so well, I leave it free—
  The scent alone I take with me !

As one who visits sacred spots
  Brings tokens back, so I from you
  A glance, a smile, a rapture new !
And these are my forget-me-nots !
  I take from you but only these—
  Give all the rest to whom you please.

Sweet eyes, your glance a light shall cast
  On me, when dreaded ghosts arise
  Of dead regrets with shrouded eyes,
And phantoms of the perished past,
  Old thoughts, old hopes, and old desire
  Gather around my lonely fire !

Farewell !   In rhyme, I kiss your hand—
  Kiss not unsweet, although unheard !—
  This is our secret—say no word—
That I have been in Fairyland,
  And seen for one brief moment's space
  The Queen Titania face to face.

NEÆRA'S WREATH

NEÆRA crowns me with a purple wreath
    That she with her own dainty hands did twine;
Gold-hearted blossoms and blue buds in sheath,
    Mingled with veined green leaves of the wild
      vine.

Then, bending down her bright head—ah, too
    nigh !—
She asks me for a song : the daylight dies :
The song is still unwritten : still I lie
    Watching the purple twilight of her eyes.

I am her laureate ; therefore heart of grace
    I take to kiss her. Where was song like this?
Love is best sung of in a loveless place,
    For who would care to sing where he might
      kiss ?

CAMILLA

CAMILLA calls me heartless : hence you see
  Logic in love has little part.
How can I otherwise than heartless be
  Seeing Camilla has my heart ?

SIXTY TO SIXTEEN

If I were young as you, Sixteen,
  And you were old as I,
I would not be as I have been,
  You would not be so shy—
We should not watch with careless mien
  The golden days go by,
If I were young as you, Sixteen,
  And you were old as I.

The years of youth are yours, Sixteen;
  Such years of old had I,
But time has set his seal between
  Dark eyebrow and dark eye.
Sere grow the leaves that once were green,
  The song turns to a sigh:
Ah! very young are you, Sixteen,
  And very old am I.

Red bloom-times come and go, Sixteen,
　With snow-soft feet, but I
Shall be no more as I have been
　In times of bloom gone by ;
For dimmer grows the pleasant scene
　Beneath the pleasant sky ;
The world is growing old, Sixteen—
　The weary world and I.

Ah, would that once again, Sixteen,
　A kissing mouth had I ;
The days would gaily go, I ween,
　Though death should stand anigh,
If springtime's green were evergreen,
　If Love would never die,
And I were young as you, Sixteen,
　And you were old as I.

BOUQUET AND BRACELET

Bouquet said : "My floral ring
  The homage of a heart encloses,
Whose thoughts to you go worshipping
  In perfume from my blushing roses."

Bracelet said : " My rubies red,
  Though hard the gleam that each exposes,
Will last when flowers of Spring are fled
  And dead are all the Summer roses."

Beauty mused awhile, and said,
  " Here's poesy !" and sighed, "Here prose is :
Bouquet ! I choose the rubies red !—
  In Winter they will buy me roses."

CUPID'S FUNERAL

By his side, whose days are past,
 Lay bow and quiver!
And his eyes that stare aghast
 Close, with a shiver.
God nor man from Death, at last,
 Love may deliver.

Though—of old—we vowed, my dear,
 Death should not take him;
Mourn not thou that we must here
 Coldly forsake him;
Shed above his grave no tear—
 Tears will not wake him.

Cupid lieth cold and dead—
  Ended his flying,
Pale his lips, once rosy-red,
  Swift was his dying.
Place a stone above his head,
  Turn away, sighing.

THE FIRST OF MAY

A MEMORY

THE waters make a music low :
    The river reeds
Are trembling to the tunes of long ago—
    Dead days and deeds

Become alive again, as on
    I float, and float,
Through shadows of the golden summers
        gone
    And springs remote.

Above my head the trees bloom out
    In white and red
Great blossoms, that make glad the air about;
    And old suns shed

Their rays athwart them.   Ah, the light
 Is bright and fair !
No suns that shine upon me now are bright
 As those suns were.

And, gazing down into the stream,
 I see a face,
As sweet as buds that blossom in a dream,
 Ere sorrows chase

Fair dreams from men, and send in lieu
 Sad thoughts.   A wreath
Of blue-bells binds the head—a bluer blue
 The eyes beneath.

This is my little Annie's face ;
 My child-sweetheart
Whom long ago I lost in that dark place
 Where all lives part.

Beside me still I see her stand,
 Who is no more.

She walked with me through childhood,
    hand in hand,
  But at the door

Of youth departed from me.   Fain
    Was I that day
To go with her.   Ah, sweetheart, come again
    This First of May!

A GHOST

Ghosts walk the Earth, that rise not from the
grave.
The Dead Past hath its living dead. We see
All suddenly, at times,—and shudder then—
Their faces pale, and sad accusing eyes.

Last night, within the crowded street, I saw
A Phantom from the Past, with pallid face
And hollow eyes, and pale, cold lips, and hair
Faded from that imperial hue of gold
Which was my pride in days that are no more.

That pallid face I knew in its young bloom—
A radiant lily with a rose-flushed heart,
Most beautiful, a vision of delight;
And seeing it again, so changed, so changed,

I felt as if the icy hand of Death
Had touched my forehead and his voice said
"Come!"

Ah, pale, cold lips that once were rosy-red!
Lips I have kissed on golden afternoons—
Past, past, and gone, and gone beyond recall—
Breathing low vows beside the summer sea
(Vows broken like the breaking of a wave);
Ah, faded hair, whose curls I have caressed,
And sworn the least of them was dearer far
Than all the wealth of all the world to me!
Ah, hollow, haunting eyes, within whose
    depths,
Flower-like, and star-like, once my Fate I saw,
Or thought I saw!—is there not any way
To call back from its grave the Buried Past?

Dear! Though my vows to thee were all for-
    sworn,
Too well, too late, I know I loved thee more
Than mine own life—a life-in-death since then.
Yet shall I nevermore in all the days

And all the lives to come, if lives there be
Beyond this life, beyond the weary earth,
Kiss thee again upon the lips and hair,
And call thee by the old caressing names,
And feel thy true heart beating against mine,
That was so false and would, too late, be true ;
For neither passionate prayer, nor burning tears,
Nor incantations that might rend the rocks,
Nor all the powers of hell, nor God Himself,
May raise the Buried Past to life again.

For thou that wert art not; dead evermore—
Dead evermore, too, that which once was I.

What exorcism will lay these haunting ghosts ?
None but a draught of the Lethean stream.
Who drinks therefrom shall all things soon
        forget,
Himself forgetting, too—the greatest good.

EVEN SO

THE days go by—the days go by,
Sadly and wearily to die :
    Each with its burden of small cares,
    Each with its sad gift of gray hairs
For those who sit, like me, and sigh,
"The days go by ! The days go by !"

Ah, nevermore on shining plumes,
Shedding a rain of rare perfumes
    That men call memories, they are borne
    As in life's many-visioned morn,
When Love sang in the myrtle-blooms—
Ah, nevermore on shining plumes !

Where is my life ? Where is my life ?
The morning of my youth was rife

With promise of a golden day.
Where have my hopes gone ?   Where are
   they—
The passion and the splendid strife?
Where is my life ?   Where is my life ?

My thoughts take hue from this wild day,
And, like the skies, are ashen gray ;
  The sharp rain, falling constantly,
  Lashes with whips of steel the sea :
What words are left for Hope to say ?
My thoughts take hue from this wild day.

I dreamt—my life is all a dream!—
That I should sing a song supreme
  To gladden all sad eyes that weep,
  And take the Harp of Time, and sweep
Its chords to some eternal theme.
I dreamt—my life is all a dream.

The world is very old and wan—
The sun that once so brightly shone

Is now as pale as the pale moon.
I would that Death came swift and soon;
For all my dreams are dead and gone.
The world is very old and wan.

. . . .

The world is young, the world is strong,
But I in dreams have wandered long.
    God lives.   What can Death do to me?
    The sun is shining on the sea.
Yet shall I sing my splendid song—
The world is young, the world is strong.

SONG

WHAT shall a man remember
  In days when he is old,
And Life is a dying ember,
  And Fame a story told?

Power—that came to leave him?
  Wealth—to the wild waves blown?
Fame—that came to deceive him?
  Ah, no! Sweet Love alone!

Honour, and Wealth, and Power
  May all like dreams depart—
But Love is a fadeless flower
  Whose roots are in the heart.

A SUNSET FANTASY

SPELLBOUND by a sweet fantasy
  At evenglow I stand
Beside an opaline strange sea
  That rings a sunset land.

The rich lights fade out one by one,
  And, like a peony
Drowning in wine, the crimson sun
  Sinks down in that strange sea.

His wake across the ocean-floor
  In a long glory lies,
Like a gold wave-way to the shore
  Of some sea paradise.

My dream flies after him, and I
   Am in another land ;
The sun sets in another sky,
   And we sit hand in hand.

Gray eyes look into mine ; such eyes
   I think the angels' are—
Soft as the soft light in the skies
   When shines the morning star,

And tremulous as morn, when thin
   Gold lights begin to glow,
Revealing the bright soul within
   As dawn the sun below.

So, hand in hand, we watch the sun
   Burn down the Western deeps,
Dreaming a charmèd dream, as one
   Who in enchantment sleeps ;

A dream of how we twain some day,
   Careless of map or chart,
Will both take ship and sail away
   Into the sunset's heart.

Our ship shall be of sandal built,
　Like ships in old-world tales,
Carven with cunning art, and gilt,
　And winged with scented sails

Of silver silk, whereon the red
　Great gladioli burn,
A rainbow-flag at her masthead,
　A rose-flag at her stern;

And, perching on the point above
　Wherefrom the pennon blows,
The figure of a flying dove,
　And in her beak a rose.

And from the fading land the breeze
　Shall bring us, blowing low,
Old odours and old memories,
　And airs of long ago—

A melody that has no words
　Of mortal speech a part,
Yet touching all the deepest chords
　That tremble in the heart:

A scented song blown oversea,
  As though from bowers of bloom
A wind-harp in a lilac-tree
  Breathed music and perfume.

And we, no more with longings pale,
  Will smile to hear it blow;
I in the shadow of the sail,
  You in the sunset-glow.

For, with the fading land, our fond
  Old fears shall all fade out,
Paled by the light from shores beyond
  The dread of Death or Doubt.

And from a gloomy cloud above
  When Death his shadow flings,
The Spirit of Immortal Love
  Will shield us with his wings.

He is the lord of dreams divine,
  And lures us with his smiles
Along the splendour opaline
  Unto the Blessed Isles.

POPPIES

THESE are the flowers of sleep
That nod in the heavy noon,
Ere the brown shades eastward creep
To a drowsy and dreamful tune—
These are the flowers of sleep.

Love's lilies are passion-pale,
But these on the sun-kissed flood
Of the corn, that rolls breast deep,
Burn redder than drops of blood
On a dead king's golden mail.

Heart's dearest, I would that we
These blooms of forgetfulness
Might bind on our brows, and steep
Our love in Lethe ere less
Grow its flame with thee or me.

When Time with his evil eye
The beautiful Love has slain,
There is nought to gain or keep
Thereafter, and all is vain.
Should we wait to see Love die?

Sweetheart, of the joys men reap
We have reaped; 'tis time to rest.
Why should we wake but to weep?
Sleep and forgetting is best—
These are the flowers of sleep.

AMARANTH

ONCE a poet—long ago—
Wrote a song as void of art
As the songs that children know,
And as pure as a child's heart.

With a sigh he threw it down,
Saying, "This will never shed
Any glory or renown
On my name when I am dead.

"I will sing a lordly song
Men shall hear, when I am gone,
Through the years sound clear and strong
As a golden clarion."

So this lordly song he sang
That would gain him deathless fame—

When the death-knell o'er him rang
No man even knew its name.

Ay, and when his way he found
To the place of singing souls,
And beheld their bright heads crowned
With song-woven aureoles,

He stood shame-faced in the throng,
For his brow of wreath was bare,
And, alas! his lordly song
Sere had grown in that sweet air;

Then, all sudden, a divine
Light fell on him from afar,
And he felt the child-song shine
On his forehead like a star.

So for ever. Each and all
Songs of passion or of mirth
That are not heart-pure shall fall
As a sky-lark's—to the earth;

But the soul's song has no bounds—
Like the voice of Israfel,
From the heaven of heavens it sounds
To the very hell of hell.

THE LITTLE PEOPLE

Who are these strange small folk,
 These that come to our homes as kings,
  Asking nor leave nor grace,
Bending our necks to their yoke,
  Taking the highest place,
 And mastery of all things ?

Whence they come none may know,
 But a wondrous land it must be ;
  Angels in exile they !
Here in this dull world below
  Creatures of sinful clay
 We feel near their purity.

Clearer their young eyes are
 Than the dew in the cups of flowers
  Gleaming, when shines at dawn,

Faintly, the morning's one star—
    Eyes whose still gaze, indrawn,
    Sees things unseen by ours.

Deep in those orbs serene—
    Little planets be-ringed and bright—
    Mysteries marvellous lie :
Known unto us they might mean
        Faith, without fear, to die,
    All sure of the waiting light.

Dimpled their hands and small—
    Would ye, therefore, their might contemn ?
    Seem they for play designed ?
Fate, and the Future withal,
        Weal, yea and Woe, of mankind,
    Lie hid in the palms of them.

Tyrants, whose terrible names
    Make men pale with affright intense,
    Worshipping, kiss their feet :
Touch of their little hands tames
        Fiercest of hearts that beat—
    So mighty is Innocence.

These are the children dear,
From a country unknown of charts :
(Dim Land of Souls Unborn),
Rosy as morn they come here,
Filling with joy forlorn
Waste places in our hearts.

A KING IN EXILE

O THE Queen may keep her golden
  Crown and sceptre of command !
I would give them both twice over
  To be King of Babyland.

Sure, it is a wondrous country
  Where the beanstalks grow apace,
And so very near the moon is
  You could almost stroke her face.

And the dwellers in that country
  Hold in such esteem their King,
They believe that if he chooses
  He can do—just anything !

And, although his regal stature
  May be only four-feet-ten,

Think him tallest, strongest, bravest,
Noblest, wisest, best of men.

Ah, how fondly I remember
The good time serene and fair,
In the bygone years when I, too,
Was a reigning monarch there !

But my subjects they discrowned me
When they'd older, colder, grown ;
And they took away my sceptre,
And upset my royal throne.

Yet, although a King in Exile,
Without subjects to command,
I am glad at heart to think I
Once was King of Babyland.

TAMERLANE

Lo, upon the carpet, where
  Throned upon a heap of slain
Blue-eyed dolls of beauty rare
  (Ah, they pleaded all in vain !)
  Sits the Infant Tamerlane !

Broken toys upon the floor
  Scattered lie—a ruined rout.
Thus from all things evermore
  Are—the fact is past a doubt—
  Hidden virtues hammered out.

Poet's page, or statesman's bust,
  Nothing comes to him amiss ;
Everything he clutches must—
  'Tis his simple dream of bliss !—
  Suffer his analysis.

O my little Tamerlane,
Infantile Iconoclast,
Is your small barbaric brain
Not o'erawed by the amassed
Wit and Wisdom of the Past?

Type are you of that which springs
Ever forth when comes the need,
Overthrowing thrones and kings,
Faithless altar, sapless creed;
Sowing fresh and living seed.

On the worn-out Roman realm,
In whose purple gnawed the moth,
Thus its pride to overwhelm,
And its state to carve like cloth,
Swept the fierce, long-sworded Goth.

Age preserves with doting care
Things from which life long has fled,
Shrieks to see Youth touch a hair
On the mouldiest mummy-head—
So Egyptians kept their dead.

Youth comes by with head high-reared,
  Stares in scorn at these august
Effigies by age revered—
  Gilded shapes of Greed and Lust—
  Shakes them into rags and dust.

Little Vandal, smash away!
  Riot while your blood is hot!—
If into the world each day
  Such as you are entered not,
  It would perish of dry-rot.

THE DEAD CHILD

ALL silent is the room,
  There is no stir of breath,
Save mine, as in the gloom
  I sit alone with Death.

Short life it had, the sweet,
  Small babe here lying dead,
With tapers at its feet
  And tapers at its head.

Dear little hands, too frail
  Their grasp on life to hold;
Dear little mouth so pale,
  So solemn, and so cold;

Small feet that nevermore
  About the house shall run;

Thy little life is o'er!
Thy little journey done!

Sweet infant, dead too soon,
Thou shalt no more behold
The face of sun or moon,
Or starlight clear and cold;

Nor know, where thou art gone,
The mournfulness and mirth
We know who dwell upon
This sad, glad, mad, old earth.

The foolish hopes and fond
That cheat us to the last
Thou shalt not feel; beyond
All these things thou hast passed.

The struggles that upraise
The soul by slow degrees
To God, through weary days—
Thou hast no part in these.

THE DEAD CHILD

And at thy childish play
  Shall we, O little one,
No more behold thee ? Nay,
  No more beneath the sun.

Death's sword may well be bared
  'Gainst those grown old in strife,
But, ah ! it might have spared
  Thy little unlived life.

Why talk as in despair ?
  Just God, whose rod I kiss,
Did not make thee so fair
  To end thy life at this.

There is some pleasant shore—
  Far from His Heaven of Pride,
Where those strong souls who bore
  His Cross in bliss abide—

Some place where feeble things,
  For Life's long war too weak,
Young birds with unfledged wings,
  Buds nipped by storm-winds bleak,

Young lambs left all forlorn
  Beneath a bitter sky,
Meek souls to sorrow born,
  Find refuge when they die.

There day is one long dawn,
  And from the cups of flowers
Light dew-filled clouds updrawn
  Rain soft and perfumed showers.

Child Jesus walketh there
  Amidst child-angel bands,
With smiling lips, and fair
  White roses in His hands.

I kiss thee on the brow,
  I kiss thee on the eyes—
Farewell! Thy home is now
  The Children's Paradise.

IN MEMORY OF AN ACTRESS

SAY little : where she lies, so let her rest :
  What cares she now for Fame, and what for
    Art ?
  What for applause ?   She has played out her
    part.
Her hands are folded calmly on her breast—
  God knows the best !

She has gone down, as all must go, to where
  The players of the past are lying low—
  Players who played their parts out long ago—
With the life-hue still bright on lips and hair
  And forehead fair.

Cheek's colour, poise of head, and flash of eye
  Who will remember them when we are dead ?
  Whom that is dead have we rememberèd ?

The end is one although we smile or sigh—
We live; we die.

Bitter to some is Death, to some is sweet—
Sweetest to youth and bitterest to age;
But simple is the costume for the stage,
The darkened stage of death, and very meet—
A winding-sheet.

So we may fill our days with grief or mirth,
Each as he pleases: but what boots it all,
When on the coffin-lid the cold clods fall,
Though we had been most eloquent on earth
Or dumb from birth?

So, let her rest who perished in her prime:
Surely through darkness she shall find the
light
And, though obscured to us in outer night,
Shall play her part yet in a play sublime
In God's good time.

THE RIVER MAIDEN

HER gown was simple woven wool,
  But, in repayment,
Her body sweet made beautiful
  The simplest raiment :

For all its fine, melodious curves
  With life a-quiver
Were graceful as the bends and swerves
  Of her own river.

Her round arms, from the shoulders down
  To sweet hands slender,
The sun had kissed them amber-brown
  With kisses tender.

For though she loved the secret shades
  Where ferns grow stilly,

And wild vines droop their glossy braids,
   And gleams the lily,

And Nature, with soft eyes that glow
   In gloom that glistens,
Unto her own heart, beating slow,
   In silence listens:

She loved no less the meadows fair,
   And green, and spacious;
The river, and the azure air,
   And sunlight gracious.

I saw her first when tender, wan,
   Green light enframed her;
And, in my heart, the Flower of Dawn
   I softly named her.

The bright sun, like a king in state,
   With banners streaming,
Rode through the fair auroral gate
   In mail gold-gleaming.

The witch-eyed stars before him paled—
So high his scorning!—
And round the hills the rose-clouds sailed,
And it was morning.

The light mimosas bended low
To do her honour,
As in that rosy morning glow
I gazed upon her.

My boat swung bowward to the stream
Where tall reeds shiver;
We floated onward, in a dream,
Far down the River.

The River that full oft has told
To Ocean hoary
A many-coloured, sweet, and old
Unending story:

The story of the tall, young trees,
For ever sighing
To sail some day the rolling seas
'Neath banners flying.

The Ocean hears, and through his caves
   Roars gusty laughter;
And takes the River, with his waves
   To roll thereafter.

But Love deep waters cannot drown;
   To its old fountains
The stream returns in clouds that crown
   Its parent mountains.

The River was to her so dear
   She seemed its daughter;
Her deep translucent eyes were clear
   As sunlit water;

And in her bright veins seemed to run,
   Pulsating, glowing,
The music of the wind and sun,
   And waters flowing.

The secrets of the trees she knew:
   Their growth, their gladness,
And, when their time of death was due,
   Their stately sadness.

Gray gums, like old men warped by time,
  She knew their story;
And theirs that laughed in pride of prime
  And leafy glory;

And theirs that, where clear waters run,
  Drooped dreaming, dreaming;
And theirs that shook against the sun
  Their green plumes gleaming.

All things of gladness that exist
  Did seem to woo her,
And well that woodland satirist,
  The lyre-bird, knew her.

And there were hidden mossy dells
  That she knew only,
Where Beauty born of silence dwells
  Mysterious, lonely.

No sounds of toil their stillness taunt,
  No hearth-smoke sullies
The air: the Mountain Muses haunt
  Those lone, green gullies.

And there they weave a song of Fate
    That never slumbers :
A song some bard shall yet translate
    In golden numbers.

A blue haze veiled the hills' huge shapes,
    A misty lustre—
Like rime upon the purple grapes,
    When ripe they cluster :

'Twas noon, and all the Vale was gold—
    An El Dorado :
The damask river seaward rolled,
    Through shine and shadow.

And, gazing on its changing glow,
    I saw, half-sighing,
The wondrous Fairyland below
    Its surface lying.

There all things shone with paler sheen ;
    More softly shimmered
The fern-fronds, and with softer green
    The myrtles glimmered :

And—like that Fisher gazing in
  The sea-depths, pining
For days gone by, who saw Julin
  Beneath him shining,

With many a wave-washed corridor,
  And sea-filled portal,
And plunged below, and nevermore
  Was seen of mortal—

So I, long gazing at the gleam
  Of fern and flower,
Felt drawn down to that World of Dream
  By magic power:

For there, I knew, in silence sat,
  With breasts slow-heaving,
Illusion's Queen Rabesquerat,
  Her web a-weaving.

But when the moon shone, large and low,
  Against Orion,
Then, as from some pale portico
  Might issue Dian,

She came through tall tree-pillars pale,
  A silver vision,
A nymph strayed out of Ida's vale
  Or fields Elysian.

While stars shone out with mystic gleams
  The woods illuming :
It seemed as if the trees in dreams
  Once more were blooming.

And all beneath those starry blooms,
  By bends and beaches,
We floated on through glassy glooms,
  Down moonlit reaches.

Ah, that was in the glad years when
  Joys ne'er were sifted,
But I on wilder floods since then
  Have darkly drifted.

Yet, River of Romance, for me
  With pictures glowing,
Through dim, green fields of Memory
  Thou still art flowing.

And still I hear, thy shores along,
 All faintly ringing,
The notes of ghosts of birds that long
 Have ceased their singing.

Was she, who then my heart did use
 To touch so purely,
A mortal maiden—or a Muse?
 I know not, surely.

But still in dreams I see her stand,
 A fairer Flora,
Serene, immortal, by the strand
 Of clear Narora.

A PICTURE

THE sun burns fiercely down the skies ;
The sea is full of flashing eyes ;
The waves glide shoreward serpentwise

And fawn with foamy tongues on stark
Gray rocks, each sharp-toothed as a shark,
And hiss in clefts and channels dark.

Blood-purple soon the waters grow,
As though drowned sea-kings fought below
Forgotten fights of long ago.

The gray owl Dusk its wings has spread;
The sun sinks in a blossom-bed
Of poppy-clouds; the day is dead.

SEA-GIFTS

Give thou a gift to me
From thy treasure-house, O sea !

Said a red-lipped laughing girl
While the summer yet was young;

And the sea laughed back and flung
At her feet a priceless pearl.

Give thou a gift to me
From thy treasure-house, O sea !

Said the maiden once again
On a night of wind and rain.

Like a ghost the moon above her
Stared through winding-sheets of cloud.

On the sand in sea-weed shroud,
Lay the pale corpse of her lover.

Which is better, gain or loss?
Which is nobler, crown or cross?

We shall know these things, maybe,
When the dead rise from the sea.

DAY AND NIGHT

Day goeth bold in cloth of gold,
  A royal bridegroom he;
But Night in jewelled purple walks—
  A Queen of Mystery.

Day filleth up his loving-cup
  With vintage golden-clear;
But Night her ebon chalice crowns
  With wine as pale as Fear.

Day drinks to Life, to ruddy Life,
  And holds a kingly feast.
Night drinks to Death; and while she
      drinks—
  Day rises in the East!

They may not meet ; they may not greet ;
   Each keeps a separate way :
Day knoweth not the stars of Night,
   Nor Night the Star of Day.

So runs the reign of Other Twain.
   Behold ! the Preacher saith
Death knoweth not the Light of Life,
   Nor Life the Light of Death !

THE POET CARE

CARE is a Poet fine :
He works in shade or shine,
And leaves—you know his sign !—
No day without its line.

He writes with iron pen
Upon the brows of men ;
Faint lines at first, and then
He scores them in again.

His touch at first is light
On Beauty's brow of white ;
The old churl loves to write
On foreheads broad and bright.

A line for young love crossed,
A line for fair hopes lost
In an untimely frost—
A line that means *Thou Wast.*

Then deeper script appears :
The furrows of dim fears,
The traces of old tears,
The tide-marks of the years.

To him with sight made strong
By suffering and wrong,
The brows of all the throng
Are eloquent with song.

VOICES

There are three mighty Voices that alway
Cry out to God to speed His Judgment Day.

The Voice of Devils, weary long ago
Of dragging souls to Everlasting Woe.

The Voice of Saints who hear, while anthems
    swell
In Heaven, the wail of sinners doomed to Hell.

The Voice of Man, sick of his desperate
Long throwing 'gainst the leaded dice of Fate.

All things are weary of the strife and stress—
In God alone is there no weariness?

THE ASCETIC

The narrow, thorny path he trod.
" Enter into My joy," said God.
The sad ascetic shook his head ;
" I've lost all taste for joy," he said.

THE SERPENT'S LEGACY.

An apple caused man's fall, as some believe ;
But that old Snake, malevolently wise,
A deadlier snare set when he left to Eve
His tongue of honey and mesmeric eyes.

HIS SOUL

ONCE from the world of living men
  I passed, by a strange fancy led,
  To a still City of the Dead,
To call upon a citizen.

He had been famous in his day;
  Much talked of, written of, and praised
  For virtues my small soul amazed—
And yet I thought his heart was clay.

He was too full of grace for me:
  His friends said, on a marble stone,
  His soul sat somewhere near the Throne:
I did not know; I called to see.

His name and fame were on the door—
A most superior tomb indeed,
Much railed, and gilt, and filagreed;
He occupied the lower floor.

I knocked—*a worm crawled from its hole :*
I looked—*and knew it for his soul.*

THE DREAM OF MARGARET

It fell upon a summer night
  The village folk were soundly sleeping,
Unconscious of the glamour white
  In which the moon all things was steeping ;
One window only showed a light ;
  Behind it, silent vigil keeping,
Sat Margaret, as one in trance—
The dark-eyed daughter of the Manse.

A flood of strange, sweet thoughts was surging
  Her passionate heart and brain within.
At last, some secret impulse urging,
  She laid aside her garment thin,
And from its snowy folds emerging,
  Like Lamia from the serpent-skin,
She stood before her mirror bright
Naked, and lovely as the night.

Her dark hair o'er her shoulders flowing
   Might well have been a silken pall
O'er Galatea's image glowing
   To life and love : she was withal—
The lamplight o'er her radiance throwing—
   With her high bosom virginal,
A woman made to madden men,
A Cleopatra born again.

Hers was the beauty dark and splendid,
   Whose spell upon the heart of man
Falls swiftly as, when day is ended,
   Night falls in lands Australian.
Her rich, ripe, scarlet lips, bow-bended,
   Smiled as such ripe lips only can ;
Her eyes, wherein strange lightnings shone,
Were deeper than Oblivion.

With round, white arms, whose warm caress
   No lover knew, raised towards the ceiling,
She looked like some young Pythoness
   The secrets dark of Fate revealing,

173

Or goddess in divine distress
To higher powers for help appealing.
This invocation, standing so,
She sang in clear, sweet tones, but low :

Soul, from this narrow,
Mean life we know,
Speed as an arrow
From bended bow !

Seek, and discover,
On land or sea,
My destined lover,
Where'er he be.

How shalt thou know him,
My heart's desire ?—
His mien will show him,
His glance of fire.

High is his bearing,
His pride is high,
His spirit daring
Burns in his eye.

Birds have done mating ;
The Spring is past ;
My arms are waiting,
My heart beats fast.

" Oh, why," she sighed, " has Fate awarded
   This lot to me whose heart is bold ?
My days by trifles are recorded,
   My suitors men whose God is gold.
Oh for the Heroes helmed and sworded,
   The lovers of the days of old,
Who broke for ladies many a lance
In gallant days of old Romance !

" Would I had lived in that great time when
   A lady's love was knight's best boon ;
When sword with sword made ringing rhyme,
      when
Mailed sea-kings fought from noon to moon,
And thought the slaughter grim no crime, when
   The prize was golden-haired Gudrun.
Then *I* might find swords, broad and bright
And keen as theirs, for me to fight.

175

"But narrow bounds my life environ,
 And hold my eager spirit in.
The men I see no heart of fire in
 Their bodies bear. My love to win
A man must have a will of iron,
 A soul of flame. Then sweet were sin
Or Death for him!" With ardent glance
Thus spake the daughter of the Manse.

Then, with a smile, she fell asleep in
 Her white and dainty maiden bed.
The chaste, cold moon alone could peep in,
 And view her tresses dark outspread
Upon an arm whose clasp might keep in
 The life of one given up for dead:
And, as she drifted down the stream
Of Slumber deep, she dreamt a dream.

 . . . .

It was a banquet rich and rare,
 The wine of France was foaming madly;
The proud and great of earth were there,
 And all were slaves to serve her gladly,

And yet on them with haughty air
  She gazed, half-scornfully, half-sadly ;
The Lady of the Feast was she—
So ran her strange dream-fantasy.

A Prince was at her fair right hand,
  And at her left a famous leader
Of hosts, with look of high command,
  And—blacker than the tents of Kedar—
An Eastern King, barbaric, grand,
  Sat near—their Queen they had decreed her.
Below the proud, the brave, the wise,
  Sat charmed by her mesmeric eyes.

Then thus she spake : " O Lords of Earth !
  Than you I know none nobler, braver;
And yet your fame, and rank, and birth,
  And wealth in *my* sight find small favour.
For all too well I know their worth—
  Long since for me they lost their savour.
The Spirit, fit to mate with mine,
Must be demoniac—or divine.

"A toast!" she cried. The gallant throng
  Sprang up, their foaming glasses clinking.
"Satan! The Spirit proud and strong!
  The bravest lover to *my* thinking!
The Wine of Life I've drunk too long:
  The Wine of death I now am drinking!" . . .
"Our Queen she was a moment since—
Bear forth the body!" said the Prince.

  .   .   .   .

A ghostly wind arose, all wet
  With tears, and full of cries and wailing,
And wringing hands, and faces set
  In bitter anguish unavailing;
It bore the soul of Margaret
  To where a voice, in tones of railing,
Cried, "Spirit proud, thou hast done well!
Thou art within the Gates of Hell!"

The soul of Margaret passed slowly,
  Yet bravely, through the Hall of Dread,
The roof whereof was hidden wholly
  By black clouds hanging overhead.

No sound disturbed the melancholy
  Deep silence—which itself seemed dead.
No wailing of the damned was heard,
No voice the fearful stillness stirred.

But that deep silence held in keeping
  The secret of Eternal Woe—
That yet seemed like a serpent creeping
  Around the walls.   It was as though
The cries of pain' and hopeless weeping
  Had died out ages long ago.
No face was seen, no figure dread. . . . .
Were all the damned and devils dead ?

No lustre known on earth was gleaming
  In that dread Hall, but some weird light
Around the pillars vast was streaming,
  And down the vistas infinite ;
A light like that men see in dreaming,
  And, waking, shudder with affright.
Its glare a baleful splendour shed
For ever through the Hall of Dread.

Then suddenly she was aware
   That from the walls, and all around her,
In motionless and burning stare,
   Millions of eyes glowed, that spellbound her;
The everlasting dumb despair
   That spoke from them made Pity founder;
And, as she passed along the floor,
She trod on burning millions more.

For floor and pillar, roof and all,
   Were full of eyes, for ever burning—
'Twas these that lit the Dreadful Hall,
   These were the damned beyond returning,
Sealed up in pillar, floor, and wall,
   Without a tongue to voice their yearning,
Or grief, or hate, so God might know :
Their eyes alone could speak their woe.

Her way lit by the weird light flowing
   From those sad, awful eyes, she passed
To where—her terror ever growing—
   Upon a Throne, in fire set fast,

And like a Rose of fire far-glowing,
  She saw a Figure, Veiled and Vast.
She trembled, for she knew full well
She stood before the Lord of Hell.

And then, an instant courage taking,
  She knelt before the burning throne;
And, all her hopes of heaven forsaking,
  She cried, "O Lord, make me thine own!
For men, though they be of God's making,
  I love not. Thee I love alone."
The figure veiled spake thus: "Arise,
O Spirit proud—and most unwise!"

And as It spake, unveiling slowly,
  A brow of awful beauty shone
On Margaret's soul—yet Melancholy
  And Woe Eternal sat thereon.
But, lo! the form was woman wholly.
  A faint smile played her lips upon,
As in a voice low, sweet, and level
She said: "My dear, I am the Devil!"

With one wild wail of bitter scorning
   The stricken soul of Margaret fled,
Sore harrowed by that dreadful warning;
   And, shrieking, through the Hall of Dread
She passed . . . and woke . . . and it was
    morning,
   And she was in her own white bed.

.   .   .   .

Soon afterwards, the tale runs, she
Took veil within a nunnery.

THE MARTYR

Not only on cross and gibbet,
  By sword, and fire, and flood,
Have perished the world's sad martyrs
  Whose names are writ in blood.

A woman lay in a hovel,
  Mean, dismal, gasping for breath ;
One friend alone was beside her—
  The name of him was—Death.

For the sake of her orphan children,
  For money to buy them food,
She had slaved in the dismal hovel
  And wasted her womanhood.

Winter and Spring and Summer
  Came each with a load of cares;
And Autumn to her brought only
  A harvest of gray hairs.

Far out in the blessèd country,
  Beyond the smoky town,
The winds of God were blowing
  Evermore up and down;

The trees were waving signals
  Of joy from the bush beyond;
The gum its blue-green banner,
  The fern its dark green frond;

Flower called to flower in whispers
  By sweet caressing names,
And young gum shoots sprang upward
  Like woodland altar-flames;

And, deep in the distant ranges,
  The magpie's fluting song
Roused musical, mocking echoes
  In the woods of Dandenong;

And riders were galloping gaily
  With loose-held flowing reins,
Through dim and shadowy gullies,
  Across broad, treeless plains;

And winds through the Heads came wafting
  A breath of life from the sea,
And over the blue horizon
  The ships sailed silently;

And out of the sea at morning
  The sun rose, golden bright,
And in crimson, and gold, and purple
  Sank in the sea at night;

But in dreams alone she saw them,
  Her hours of toil between;
For life to her was only
  A heartless dead machine.

Her heart was in the graveyard
  Where lay her children three,
Nor work nor prayer could save them,
  Nor tears of agony.

On the lips of her last and dearest
  Pressing a farewell kiss,
She cried aloud in her anguish—
  " Can God make amends for *this* ?"

Dull, desperate, ceaseless slaving
  Bereft her of power to pray,
And Man was careless and cruel,
  And God was far away.

But who shall measure His mercies ?
  His ways are in the deep ;
And, after a life of sorrow,
  He gave her His gift of sleep.

Rest comes at last to the weary,
  And freedom to the slave ;
Her tired and worn-out body
  Sleeps well in its pauper grave.

But His angel bore her soul up
  To that Bright Land and Fair,
Where Sorrow enters never,
  Nor any cloud of Care.

They came to a lovely valley,
 Agleam with asphodel,
And the soul of the woman speaking
 Said—" Here I fain would dwell ! "

The Angel answered gently :
 " O Soul most pure and dear,
O Soul most tried and truest,
 Thy dwelling is not here !

" Behold thy place appointed—
 Long kept, long waiting—come !—
Where bloom on the hills of heaven
 The roses of Martyrdom ! "

HIS MATE

It may have been a fragment of that higher
  Truth dreams, at times, disclose;
It may have been to Fond Illusion nigher—
  But thus the story goes:

A fierce sun glared upon a gaunt land, stricken
  With barrenness and thirst,
Where Nature's pulse with joy of Spring would
    quicken
  No more; a land accurst.

Gray salt-bush grimmer made the desolation—
  Like mocking immortelles
Strewn on the graveyard of a perished nation
  Whose name no record tells.

No faintest sign of distant water glimmered
  The aching eye to bless;
The far horizon like a sword's edge shimmered,
  Keen, gleaming, pitiless.

And all the long day through the hot air
    quivered
  Beneath a burning sky,
In dazzling dance of heat that flashed and
    shivered:
  It seemed as if hard by

The borders of this region, evil-favoured,
  Life ended, Death began:
But no; upon the plain a shadow wavered—
  The shadow of a man.

What man was this by Fate or Folly driven
  To cross the dreadful plain?
A pilgrim poor? or Ishmael unforgiven?
  The man was Andy Blane,

A stark old sinner, and a stout, as ever
  Blue swag has carried through

That grim, wild land men name the Never-Never,
  Beyond the far Barcoo.

His strength was failing now, but his unfailing
  Strong spirit still upbore
And drove him on with courage yet unquailing,
  In spite of weakness sore.

When, lo! beside a clump of salt-bush lying,
  All suddenly he found
A stranger, who before his eyes seemed dying
  Of thirst, without a sound.

Straightway beside that stranger on the sandy
  Salt plain—a death-bed sad—
Down kneeling, "Drink this water, mate!" said
      Andy—
  It was the last he had.

Behold a miracle! for when that Other
  Had drunk, he rose and cried,
"Let us pass on!" As brother might with
      brother
  So went they, side by side;

Until the fierce sun, like an eyeball bloody
  Eclipsed in death, was seen
No more, and in the spacious West, still
  ruddy,
  A star shone out serene.

As one, then, whom some memory beguiling
  May gladden, yea, and grieve,
The stranger, pointing up, said, sadly smiling,
  " The Star of Christmas Eve ! "

Andy replied not.   Unto him the sky was
  All reeling stars ; his breath
Came thick and fast ; and life an empty lie was ;
  True one thing only—Death.

  .   .   .   .

Beneath the moonlight, with the weird, wan
    glitter
  Of salt-bush all around,
He lay ; but by his side in that dark, bitter,
  Last hour, a friend he found.

"Thank God!" he said.   "*He's* acted more
    than square, mate,
By me in this—and *I'm*
A Rip. . . . He must have known I was—well,
    there, mate—
A White Man all the time.

"To-morrow's Christmas day : God knows where
    I'll be
By then—I don't ; but you
Away from this Death's hole should many a mile
    be,
At Blake's, on the Barcoo.

"You take this cheque there—they will cash it,
    sonny. . . . .
It meant my Christmas spree . . . .
And do just what you like best with the money,
    In memory of me."

The stranger, smiling, with a little leaven
    Of irony, said, "Yea,

But *there* it shall not be.   With *me* in Heaven
   You'll spend your Christmas Day."

Then that gray heathen, that old back-block
      stager,
   Half-jestingly replied,
And laughed—and laughed again—"Mate, it's
      a wager!"
And, grimly laughing, died.

.   .   .   .

St. Peter stood at the Celestial Portal,
   Gazing down gulfs of air,
When Andy Blane, no longer now a mortal,
   Appeared before him there.

" What seek'st thou here?" the saint in tone
      ironic
   Said. " Surely the wrong gate
This is for thee."   Andy replied, laconic,
   "I want to find my mate."

M   193

The gates flew wide. The glory unbeholden
  Of mortal eyes was there.
He gazed—this trembling sinner—at the golden
  Thrones, terrible and fair,

And shuddered. Then down through the living
    splendour
  Came One unto the gate
Who said, with outspread hands, in accents
    tender:
  "Andy! *I* am your mate!"

THE OLD WIFE AND THE NEW

Hɪ sat beneath the curling vines
    That round the gay verandah twined,
His forehead seamed with sorrow's lines,
    An old man with a weary mind.

His young wife, with a rosy face
    And brown arms ambered by the sun,
Went flitting all about the place—
    Master and mistress both in one.

What caused that old man's look of care ?
    Was she not blithe and fair to see ?
What blacker than her raven hair,
    What darker than her eyes might be ?

The old man bent his weary head ;
    The sunlight on his gray hair shone ;

His thoughts were with a woman dead
   And buried, years and years agone :

The good old wife who took her stand
   Beside him at the altar-side,
And walked with him, hand clasped in hand,
   Through joy and sorrow till she died.

Ah, she was fair as heart's desire,
   And gay, and supple-limbed, in truth,
And in his veins there leapt like fire
   The hot red blood of lusty youth.

She stood by him in shine and shade,
   And, when hard-beaten at his best,
She took him like a child and laid
   His aching head upon her breast.

She helped him make a little home
   Where once were gum-trees gaunt and stark,
And bloodwoods waved green-feathered foam—
   Working from dawn of day to dark,

Till that dark forest formed a frame
    For vineyards that the gods might bless,
And what was savage once became
    An Eden in the wilderness.

And how at their first vintage-time
    She laughed and sang—you see such shapes
On vases of the Grecian prime—
    And danced a reel upon the grapes!

And ever, as the years went on,
    All things she kept with thrifty hand,
Till never shone the sun upon
    A fairer homestead in the land.

Then children came—ah, me! ah, me!
    Sad blessings that a mother craves!
That old man from his seat could see
    The shadows playing o'er their graves.

And then she closed her eyes at last,
    Her gentle, useful, peaceful life

Was over—garnered with the past;
God rest thee gently, Good Old Wife!

.   .   .   .

His young wife has a rosy face,
    And laughs, with reddest lips apart,
But cannot fill the empty place
    Within that old man's lonely heart.

His young wife has a rosy face,
    And brown arms ambered by the sun,
Goes flitting all about the place,
    Master and mistress both in one;

But though she sings, or though she sighs,
    He sees her not—he sees instead
A gray-haired Shade with gentle eyes—
    The good old wife, long dead, long dead.

He sits beneath the curling vines,
    Through which the merry sunrays dart,
His forehead seamed with sorrow's lines—
    An old man with a broken heart.

A CHRISTMAS EVE

Good fellows are laughing and drinking
  (To-night no heart should grieve),
But I am of old days thinking,
  Alone, on Christmas Eve.
Old memories fast are springing
  To life again; old rhymes
Once more in my brain are ringing—
  Ah, God be with old times!

There never was man so lonely
  But ghosts walked him beside,
For Death our spirits can only
  By veils of sense divide.
Numberless as the blades of
  Grass in the fields that grow,

Around us hover the shades of
The dead of long ago.

Friends living a word estranges;
We smile, and we say "Adieu!"
But, whatsoever else changes,
Dead friends are faithful and true.
An old-time tune, or a flower,
The simplest thing held dear
In bygone days has the power
Once more to bring them near.

And whether it be through thinking
Of memories sad and sweet,
Or hearing the cheery clinking
Of glasses across the street,
I know not; but this is certain
That, here in the dusk, I view
Like shadows seen through a curtain,
The shades of the friends I knew.

Methinks that I hear their laughter—
An echo of ghostly mirth,

As if in the dim Hereafter
  They jest as they did on earth.
The fancy possibly droll is,
  And yet it relieves my mind
To think the enfranchised soul is
  So humorously inclined.

But hark! whose steps in the glancing
  Moonbeams are these I hear,
That sound as if timed to dancing
  Music of gallant cheer!
Half Galahad, half Don Juan,
  His head full of wild romance;
'Twas thus that of old would Spruhan
  Come lilting, "We met by chance."

Sure never a spirit lighter
  At heart quaffed mountain dew;
Never was goblin brighter
  That Oberon's kingdom knew.
And though at this season yearly
  I miss the grasp of his hand,

I know that Spruhan has merely
Gone back to Fairyland.

. . . .

The shades grow dimmer and dimmer,
  And now they fade from view,
I see in the East the glimmer
  Of dawn.   Old friends, adieu !
Sitting here, lonely hearted,
  Writing these random rhymes,
I drink to the days departed,—
  Ah, God be with old times !

NIGHT

The Night is young yet; an enchanted night
In early summer : calm and darkly bright.

I love the Night, and every little breeze
She brings, to soothe the sleep of dreaming
trees.

Hearst thou the Voices? Sough! Susurrus!—
Hark!
'Tis Mother Nature whispering in the dark!

Burden of cities, mad turmoil of men,
That vex the daylight—she forgets them then.

Her breasts are bare; Grief gains from them
surcease :
She gives her restless sons the milk of Peace.

To sleep she lulls them—drawn from thoughts
   of pelf—
By telling sweet old stories of herself.

.   .   .   .

All secrets deep—yea, all I hear and see
Of things mysterious—Night reveals to me.

I know what every flower, with drowsy head
Down-drooping, dreams of—and the seeming
   dead.

I know how they, escaped from care and strife,
Ironically moralise on Life.

And know what—when the moon walks on the
   waves—
They whisper to each other in their graves.

I know that white clouds drifting from stark
   coasts
Across the sky at midnight are the ghosts

Of sailors drowned at sea, who yearn to win
A quiet grave beside their kith and kin

In still green graveyards, where they lie at ease
Far from the sound of surge and roar of seas.

I know the message of the mournful rain
That beats upon the widow's window-pane.

I know the meaning of the roar of seas ;
I know the glad Spring sap-song of the trees ;

And that great chant to which in tuneful grooves
The green round earth upon its axis moves ;

And that still greater chant the Bright Sun
    sings—
Fire-crowned Apollo—the great chant that brings

All things to life, and draws through spaces dim,
And star-sown realms, his planets after him.

1 know the tune that led, since Life began,
The upward, downward, onward March of Man.

I hear the whispers that the Angels twain
Of Death and Life exchange in meeting—fain

Are they to pause and greet, yet may not stay.
"Never!"   "For ever."   This is all they say.

I hear the twitterings inarticulate
Of souls unborn that press around the Gate

Of Birth, each striving which shall first escape
From formless vapour into human shape.

I know the tale the bird of passionate heart,
The nightingale, tries ever to impart

To men, though vainly—for I well believe
That in her brown breast beats the heart of Eve,

Who with her sweet, sad, wistful music tries
To tell her sons of their lost Paradise,

And solemn secrets Man had grace to know,
When God walked in the Garden long ago.

. . . .

Yea, I have seen, methought, on nights of awe,
The vision terrible Lucretius saw :

The trembling Universe—suns, stars, grief,
   bliss—
Plunging for ever down a black abyss.

But more I love good Bishop Jeremy,
Who likens all the star-worlds that we see—

Which seem to run an everlasting race—
Unto a snowstorm sweeping on through space.

Suns, planets, stars, in glorious array
They march, melodious, on their unknown way.

Thought, seraph-winged and swifter than the
   light,
Unto the dim verge of the Infinite,

Pursues them, through that strange ethereal
   flood
In which they swim (mayhap it is the blood

Of Universal God wherein they are
But corpuscles—sun, satellite, and star—

And their great stream of glory but a dim,
Small pulse in the remotest vein of Him)

Pursues in vain, and from lone, awful glooms
Turns back to earth again with weary plumes.

.   .   .   .

Through glacial gulfs of Space the soul must
    roam
To feel the comfort of its earthly home.

Ah, Mother dear! broad-bosomed Mother Earth!
Mother of all our Joy, Grief, Madness, Mirth!—

Mother of flower and fruit, of stream and sea!—
We are thy children and must cling to thee.

I lay my head upon thy breast and hear—
Small, small and faint, yet strangely sweet and
    clear—

The hum and clash of little worlds below,
Each on its own path moving, swift or slow.

And listening, ever with intenter ear,
Through din of wars invisible I hear

A Homer—genius is not gauged by mass—
Singing his Iliad on a blade of grass.

And nations hearken : his great song resounds
Unto the tussock's very utmost bounds.

States rise and fall, each blade of grass upon,
But still his song from blade to blade rolls on

Through all the tussock-world, and Helen still
Is Fairest Fair, and Ajax wild of will—

An Ajax whose huge size, when measured o'er,
Is full ten-thousandth of an inch or more—

Still hurls defiance at the gods whose home
Is in the distant, awful, dew-drop dome

That trembling hangs, suspended from a spray,
An inch above him—worlds of space away.

Old prophecies foretell—but Time proves all—
The day will come when it, like Troy, shall fall.

Lo! through this small great wondrous song
there runs
The marching melody of stars and suns.

   .   .   .   .

I know these things, yet cannot speak and tell
Their meanings.   Over all is cast a spell.

Secrets they are, sealed with a sevenfold seal;
My soul knows what my tongue may not reveal.

   .   .   .

I love the Night!   Bright Day the soul shuts in;
Night sends it soaring to its starry kin.

If I must leave at last my place of birth—
This homely, gracious, green, familiar Earth,

With all it holds of sorrow and delight—
I pray my parting-hour may be at night,

And that her curtain dark may softly fall
On scenes I love, ere I depart from all.

Then shall I haply, journeying through the Vast
Mysterious Silences, take one long, last

Fond look at Earth, and watch from depths afar
The dear old planet dwindling to a star;

And sigh farewell unto the friends of yore,
Whose kindly faces I shall see no more.

www.ingramcontent.com/pod-product-compliance
Lightning Source LLC
Chambersburg PA
CBHW030123030726
47498CB00007B/2520